Bad Girl Publishing Presents:

You Did Me Dirty: You Reap What You Sow!

By: Authoress Tiffany Gilbert

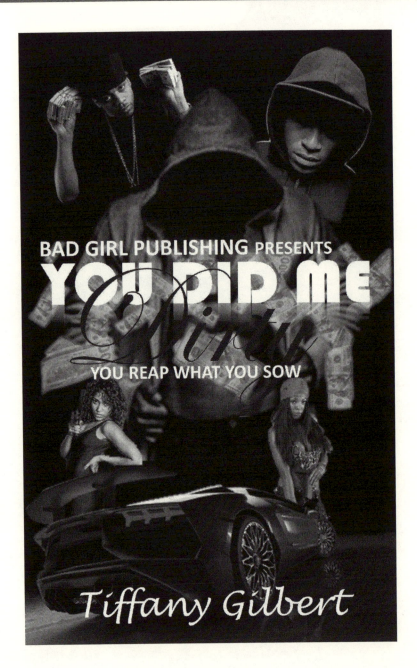

YOU DID ME DIRTY: YOU REAP WHAT YOU SOW!

Copyright 2019 Bad Girl Publishing

All rights reserved no parts of this book may be reproduced in any form without written permission/ consent from the author, except brief quotes used in reviews. This is an original work of fiction. Any references or similarities to actual events, real people, living or dead, or to real locals are intended to give the novel a sense of reality. Any similarity in other names, characters, places and incidents are entirely coincidental.

Acknowledgements

I would like to first give all thanks to my father the man above God, without God giving me this talent to be able to write books and put my words together I wouldn't be the author I am today. I would also love to give a major shout out to my parents Martha and Leroy. I would love to give a shout to my husband Deshawn Gilbert. I would love to shout out all of my sisters Lisa, Elizabeth and my brother Kevin. I would love to shout out my nieces and nephews Laquitia, Dominique, Aubree, Alonzo, Carlos, Kenya. I would love to shout out my god parents Mr. and Mrs. Renfroe, Mrs. Betty Harris May you rest peacefully, Faye Pittman and Connie Wilkins.

I would love to say thank you to my God sisters Nellie, Tracey, Niqua, Cherelle. My best friends Latoya and Cheyenne. I would love to say thank you to Kandy (Krystal) for always standing behind me girl two years since I met you thank you for the covers they are always dope. I would love to say thank you to Erika for stay real and loyal my pen sister for life we locked in. I would love to thank my authors the bad girls behind the pens at Bad Girl Publishing Raven, Cheyenne, Chrischelle you three rock we have an unbreakable bond thank y'all for giving me a chance.

YOU DID ME DIRTY: YOU REAP WHAT YOU SOW!

I would also like to thank Everybody who has ever picked up a copy of my books rather it was online on amazon or a paper back. I appreciate everyone because being an author/ publisher is not easy it come with long days, long hours. God Bless everyone who support me and who support Bad Girl Publishing as a movement.

YOU DID ME DIRTY: YOU REAP WHAT YOU SOW!

Synopsis

Being a top notch, boss chick Myesha never needed a man for anything because she is self-made. Falling in love with Jackson was genuine and although they had their problems she stuck by his side. Jackson has grown since he has met Myesha. One thing that hasn't changed is his playboy attitude. Niomi is the side chick that is good at keeping a secret that is until Jackson's careless ways gets him caught up. Niomi has been seeing Jackson on the low and he pays for everything. She is a boss working the pole at night and going to school during the day. She is working hard to become a LPN and with Jackson taking care of her she will reach her goals. Saccora is Niomi cousin/best friend. She is a sac chaser and also dates one of Jackson's enemies, Boogie. Ever since the night of Big B's party Boogie has been keeping a secret and it is tearing him apart. His carelessness caused heartache and because he doesn't know how to deal he takes it out the wrong person. With so much drama going with this twisted plot you will have to keep. Who did who wrong and who will reap what they sow? Find out in this page turner.

YOU DID ME DIRTY: YOU REAP WHAT YOU SOW!

Chapter One

Myesha

"Sex with me is amazing stay up out of my Instagram with your temptation." I swayed to the sounds of Rhianna while I sing along to the music.

I was feeling myself while sipping on my wine. Jackson had just left our house to go take care of some business, so he said. I had been with Jackson for the last four years and it hasn't been the best four years. I met Jackson one day shopping, I thought he was single when I say he laid that sweet talk on me and as gullible as I was back then I dropped my panties right along with my morals. One year into messing with Jackson I got a phone call from his wife, that's right I said it this nigga was married to some girl named Shelly. Shelly and Jackson had been together for six years. I had no clue that Jackson was married hell we had an apartment together at the time, so I didn't even think that I was actually the side bitch, but now that I think about it there were times when Jackson didn't come home at night but you know how dope niggas are it's always the streets, so I chalked it up to my nigga was

YOU DID ME DIRTY: YOU REAP WHAT YOU SOW!

telling the truth. I guess you can say the materialistic things clouded my fucken judgement.

Back to Shelly, well Shelly kept it sweet and simple that day on the phone. I felt stupid as hell, but she didn't blame me, she blamed Jackson. She let it be known right then and there she didn't want anything to do with Jackson and she was done playing games with him while he continued to hoe around in the streets and make her feel like a fool. I was shocked because I felt like this woman was trying to give me her fucken problems. I wasn't built to be nobodies side bitch even though Jackson had made me out to be one without my permission and without telling me he was married. Here I was thinking I had myself a good nigga and had him all to myself and I was a fucken home wrecker. My phone rung and took me out of my thoughts as I thought back to the beginning of my first of many fuck ups with Jackson. I looked at the screen and it was none other than my home girl Amber.

"Wass Up girl?" I said sipping this wine.

"Girl, nothing thinking about hitting the bar tonight. You down, you not doing nothing but sitting on that couch collecting checks bitch." Amber said being smart.

YOU DID ME DIRTY: YOU REAP WHAT YOU SOW!

Smacking my lips. "Shit, girl it don't matter what I'm doing. I'm minding my business, but I'll roll out who driving let me guess me since you drove last time." I said already knowing before she even answered.

"Girl, you can drive your right I drove the last time. What time are we leaving? We going to floods I didn't tell you that Big B was having a birthday party down there tonight." Amber said all in one breath.

"Ok, I knew I was driving but I'll be there at ten and be ready don't keep me waiting or I will leave your ass. Fuck bitch that should have been the first thing you mentioned when you said we were going out. Your trying to get some shit started tonight you know Jackson is going to be there they cool." I said frustrated.

"Girl, I will be ready and bitch it don't matter we are going out we don't go to be there for nobody. Ain't nobody thinking about Jackson he go out all the time you act like you can't go nowhere." Amber said smacking her lips.

"Girl now you know my nigga is off limits and we don't talk about what he do period, but I will see you at ten." I said hanging up before she could respond.

YOU DID ME DIRTY: YOU REAP WHAT YOU SOW!

Getting off the phone with Amber her hot ass know she know how to work my fucken nerves. Talking to her ass I had finished half of the bottle of wine I was drinking, and I was feeling good as fuck too. I put my phone back on the charger, grabbed my bottle and went to my room it was already eight pm, so I only had an hour to get ready. I had been lounging around at home all day still in my robe after Jackson had dicked me down this morning before leaving. I walked into my bathroom and ran me some bath water. I threw some lavender bath beads and bath gel in the water. Lavender always made me feel pure and made my body soft. I had thought about what I wanted to put on the weather wasn't too cold and it wasn't too hot, so I had the perfect outfit. I pulled out my blue jean button up shirt, with my blue jean booty shorts with the rips all in the back and front. I had paired them with some Givenchy sheer tights with some Givenchy shoe boots. I thought the fit was fire I knew I was going to be the shit tonight.

I knew once Jackson saw my outfit, he might be mad because he was going to be there tonight, so I was pushing it with these shorts. I went into the bathroom and hopped in the tub and relaxed and soaked my body and finished off the last of my bottle of wine. After about thirty minutes I washed my body and got out. I wrapped the towel

YOU DID ME DIRTY: YOU REAP WHAT YOU SOW!

around my body, when I got to my room Jackson was coming in the room looking good. From the look on his face I already knew he was about to start some shit I was just waiting on him to open his fucken mouth.

"Myesha why you got the music so loud, you couldn't even hear me come in with that shit so loud. You not even paying attention to the camera I could have been anybody you are tripping you not on your shit." Jackson said obviously pissed.

"Jackson the music is not loud, don't come in here with all that shit after you been gone all fucken day, move the fuck around yo." I said grabbing my undergarments.

"I don't know what have gotten into you lately. You always flip at the mouth and you keep an attitude unless I'm handing you that cash or that dick." Jackson said with a smirk on his face.

I didn't find shit funny I was about to check his ass. "First off Jackson let's keep it real nigga I had my own money when I met your ass. I never needed you for shit my nigga that you got wrong, yeah the dick good but don't flatter your fucken self they make fake dicks all day my nigga." I said brushing past him, but I stopped because he smelled like a bitch perfume.

YOU DID ME DIRTY: YOU REAP WHAT YOU SOW!

"Yeah, ok you got it you had your own money but don't act like a nigga have never invested in your ass." Jackson said.

"You need to go wash your ass while you coming in here smelling like a bitch with that cheap ass perfume." I said trying to leave but he grabbed my hand.

"You act like I don't stay here I can come here when I please I pay the bills here. I don't smell like a bitch I been out hustling and taking care of business all day. Where you think you going got clothes laid out and shit." Jackson looking like he was hurt after I said the shit I said.

"Out with Amber to mind my fucken business do you mind." I said

"Yeah, ok let me find out you are fucking around on a nigga I'm going to kill your ass." Jackson said.

I didn't even respond to the shit he was talking at least once a month whenever I got ready to go out Jackson always threw these threats out. I finished putting my clothes on and I grabbed my keys and purse and by then Jackson had gotten in the shower.

Chapter Two

Jackson

I'm Jackson and I know my baby Myesha told y'all what she wanted Y'all to know about me. Myesha wanted to make a nigga look bad I already know. I know I was wrong for never telling Myesha I was married when I first met her, but it wasn't like I was hiding the shit, I just wasn't a nigga who was out in the open with his shit. I never expected Shelly wacky ass to call Myesha and blow my shit up like that. The real story is me and Shelly had been separated and even though we were still living together we weren't together in a relationship. I cheated on Shelly but that wasn't until Shelly killed my seed that she was pregnant with. I never forgave Shelly I had long fell out of love with Shelly. Shelly was a bad ass light bright ass bitch that I met before I got into the game. Long after the money, materialistic shit and the fame of being with a dope boy changed her. Shelly lost her ways; she was stealing my coke sniffing my shit and for a long time I

YOU DID ME DIRTY: YOU REAP WHAT YOU SOW!

ignored the face that my bitch was turning into a cokehead truth of the matter is I was blinded by love and the good pussy between her legs.

When I fell out of love with Shelly there were many hoes, but that was until I met Myesha. Myesha seemed to have all the qualities a real nigga needed. Myesha was bad and had a body, wide hips, thin ass waist, big apple bottom with a nice set of breasts to match. Myesha hair was all real it was hanging down her back she had that good shit. Myesha rocked bundles sometimes and make up but most of all she was all natural most of the times. When I met Myesha she had just opened up her first boutique on the east side off eight mile and was about to open up her second spot over on the west side off Livernois. The thing that stood between Myesha and Shelly was Shelly didn't do nothing but spend my money and look good all day, where Myesha was her own boss and made her own money, that was what I loved the most about Myesha that was my baby. When Myesha decided she wanted to sell bundles to local beauty shops, I funded that shit even though she didn't need me to do a damn thing, but I wanted too.

The first year me and Myesha was together I fucked up and I been trying to gain her trust back since the shit happened with Shelly. I still had my share of hoes one I was messing with Naomi, a bad dark

YOU DID ME DIRTY: YOU REAP WHAT YOU SOW!

skin bitch that stripped down at Erotic City. I fucked with her because she played her position well, she never nagged me not saying that Myesha nags me I'm just a nigga in the game who can have his share of bitches. Naomi always drained my dick whenever I needed her too and I always left her a few bills to go shopping or something. Tonight, a homie of mines names Big B was having a birthday party down at floods, so you know me, and my crew was down to roll. I didn't trust that nigga Big B as far as I could throw his ass. My niggas Josh and Landon was rolling with me tonight. When I got home Myesha had the music loud as hell and from the looks of things she was on her way out as well. She was coming out the bathroom when I walked into the room, she was looking good enough to eat had Naomi not just drained my dick I would have dropped all ten inches of dick into Myesha especially for being so flip at the mouth.

When I got out the shower Myesha was gone and I guess she couldn't wait on a nigga. I had just finished getting dressed when my phone rung. I had to pinch the bridge of my nose it was my ex-wife Shelly calling to irritate me. Shelly only call when she want money or dick and she wasn't getting the dick so she could use that against me. Shelly couldn't stomach the fact that I wasn't running up behind her ass

YOU DID ME DIRTY: YOU REAP WHAT YOU SOW!

and that I was still with Myesha even after she told Myesha about me and her being married. Shelly was just salty as fuck basically because a nigga had moved on. I started to let the phone go to voice mail but decided to see what this bitch had to say today. Remember I told you the bitch was a coke head, so I already knew her.

"What the fuck do you want Shelly?" I said.

"Don't what the fuck me Jackson. I asked you to drop me off some money so that I could pay my bills." Shelly said.

"I asked you to get a fucken job Shelly. We been divorced for three years the only reason I was still looking out for you was because of our history. But baby girl you about to be thirty-five years old grow the fuck up and be a grown ass woman." I said snapping.

"I am grown Jackson do you tell that bitch Myesha that shit too. I bet you don't so run me my money nigga." Shelly said like she was mad.

"I don't have to tell Myesha shit and what I tell you about putting her name in your mouth. Myesha don't stay in my pockets my bitch a boss on her own and don't need me for shit furthermore I'm not running you shit now bye bitch." I said hanging up.

I hung up right in Shelly face this was an occurring thing. I don't know where I went wrong with Shelly. I didn't see the laziness at

YOU DID ME DIRTY: YOU REAP WHAT YOU SOW!

first. I enjoyed taking care of my wife but that bitch just didn't have any drive at all that's what turned me off. I was about five minutes from floods and downtown was packed as hell tonight. Pulling up to the valet I handed the guy my keys to my 2019 S- Class. I never paid a cover charge, so I walked right into the bar with my gun as well. My niggas was already in V.I.P waiting on me as I was walking, I saw that nigga Big B in his area I threw my hand up and went on about my business.

"Yo, my nigga it's about time you made it here. I saw Myesha and Amber on the other side in V.I.P. That nigga Landon over there in Amber face as usual." Josh said dapping me up.

"Shit, my nigga I had to go home and shower, you know I was fucking with Nioma ol wet pussy ass earlier. That nigga Landon don't never stop trying to spit game at Amber ass." I said. Sitting down.

"My nigga when you get here." Landon said walking up.

"Just now nigga wass up." I said dapping him up.

"Shit, I saw that nigga Ty smiling all in Myesha face before I went over there to kick it with Amber fine ass." Landon said.

"Word let me go check her ass she dun lost her shit tonight." I said walking away.

YOU DID ME DIRTY: YOU REAP WHAT YOU SOW!

I was pissed but didn't show it, one thing I'm big on is Respect and Loyalty and Myesha was tripping letting that nigga Ty smile all in her face like I wasn't shit or like she didn't know I was going to be in the building. I'm a known ass nigga in Detroit and Myesha knew that. When I walked up in Myesha area she was sitting there drinking Moet like the boss bitch that she was. She didn't look surprised to see me standing there she had a smirk on her face like some shit was funny.

"Yo, let me holla at you Myesha." I said yelling over the loud music. Smacking her lips standing up. "Wassup Jackson why you looked pissed off you knew I was going to be here tonight. Please don't blow my buzz with your bull shit." Myesha said with her hands on her wide hips.

"What the fuck that nigga Ty doing smiling in your face. You got a nigga that shit disrespectful as fuck make me fuck you up Myesha." I said with a scowl on my face.

"He was just speaking making sure me and Amber was good tell your fucking reporter I'm a grown ass woman and next time ask me don't assume shit going on over this way." Myesha said walking back to her seat flagging down the waitress.

YOU DID ME DIRTY: YOU REAP WHAT YOU SOW!

Pissed wasn't the word Myesha had never dismissed me like that. I went back to my area as if nothing even happened, but this conversation wasn't over. I was about to nip whatever was going on in the bud tonight with Myesha ass. I could see Myesha and Amber they looked as if they were having the best time of, they life. About an hour after being there a waitress came over with two buckets with bottles. We had a table full of bottles already, so I wasn't sure where this came from.

"Shorty, we didn't order anymore bottles you can take that back to the bar where did this shit come from." I said looking at the waitress.

"I'm sorry I know you didn't order these but the woman on the other side over there said send you two personal bottles of your favorite drink and it was on her." The waitress said.

I looked in the direction of where she pointed and sure enough my baby was on her boss shit tonight. She had sent over a bottle of DOM and a bottle of Remy Martin Louis Xii Cognac. It was just like her to send me a bottle Myesha was a boss and she knew it that was one reason why I loved her. I didn't see a bitch messing with her in Detroit she was the baddest bitch I seen who had all her shit together it still

YOU DID ME DIRTY: YOU REAP WHAT YOU SOW!

didn't stop the fact that Ty bitch ass was in my woman face. The party was lit as fuck I was enjoying myself and I was drunk as shit. I saw Myesha and Amber get up and dance a few times, but I already knew Myesha was on her shit and she wasn't the partying type at all. Myesha was like me she chilled and made sure her surroundings was in order before having fun she never wanted to be caught slipping because of who I was in the streets everybody knew she was my woman and you know how the streets is if they can't get you they will get the person closer to you. I was enjoying myself so much when I looked up Naomi was walking up to my section. I knew shit was about to hit the fucken fan she was supposed to be at work tonight not down here at Big B party. I had to get her ass out of here or Myesha was going to drag her ass and I couldn't have that shit or my shit blowing up like this. Pulling out my phone texting Naomi before she could get any further into the area. I had Josh tell her she couldn't come up in this area because I didn't want any problems. Naomi would understand she knew better.

Me: Naomi baby what you are doing here you supposed to be at work. You know I can't have you in my area my woman here tonight she will clown if she saw your ass here.

YOU DID ME DIRTY: YOU REAP WHAT YOU SOW!

Naomi: Baby my bad I didn't know your girl was here I just saw you and was coming to speak. The club was dead as hell because everybody was down here, I only stopped by for a drink or two then I was going home. I got class in the morning so I'm kind of tired.

Me: Damn I didn't know the club was dead baby I'll stop by tomorrow and drop you off a few stacks from what you missed tonight. Yeah you go home you know what you got to do and only two drinks.

Naomi didn't reply I actually saw her throw two shots back and she was out the door just that quick. When I looked up and over at Myesha area I saw her and Amber throwing shots back and the look on her face told me she thought I was up to some bull shit. My niggas was having the time of they life it was all kind of bitches in our area, but I didn't even get into all that because I knew what kind of static would be once I got back home. A nigga was tied I had been out all damn day and night. I caught a glimpse of Myesha and Amber making their way towards the door. I saw Ty grab Myesha arm and seen the scowl on her face which meant she wasn't happy about him putting his hands on her.

"Yo, let me go put this nigga Ty in his place for putting his hands on Myesha." I said to Josh and Landon.

YOU DID ME DIRTY: YOU REAP WHAT YOU SOW!

"Let's go then nigga these niggas think they can violate." Josh said.

Walking through the club trying to get to Myesha and Amber who didn't see me or my niggas coming and I'm sure Ty didn't either because he was engrossed in whatever he was saying to Myesha. "Aye Ty get your fucken hands off my woman before we have some problems here." I said standing in his face.

"Nigga you don't want these problems I didn't know that she was your woman." Ty said.

I laughed and socked his ass." Bull shit my nigga you knew this was my woman everybody in Detroit know that Myesha was my woman." I said stomping Ty ass out.

"Stop Jackson just stop let's just go please." Myesha said yelling.

"Go home Myesha now!" I yelled.

"Nigga what you not going to do is be yelling at me like I'm one these hoe ass niggas." Myesha said getting mad.

"Myesha, baby I said go on home now don't make me say it again." I said.

YOU DID ME DIRTY: YOU REAP WHAT YOU SOW!

"Fuck you Jackson it wasn't that serious" Myesha said walking away with Amber.

When I looked over my shoulder, I saw Myesha and Amber were gone out the club. Big B had come over and tried to intervene and My niggas wasn't having that shit. Floods was in an uproar when one of Big B niggas starting shooting in the club. Me and my niggas got the fuck out of the club and quick. Our cars were already waiting on us outside, so we jumped in our shit and left. I knew this shit was far from over so I knew I would have to be on my shit from here on out me and my team. I pulled up at home and I saw Myesha car wasn't in the garage or outside of the garage, so I pulled in and went into the house. I jumped in the shower and laid my ass down I must have dozed off because I never heard Myesha come in the house.

Chapter Three

The Wrong Vibes

When I had gotten home, I saw Jackson was already home and had beat me. I hated whenever me and Jackson was in the same building together because things could go left really quick if he felt disrespect from someone else. I knew coming here tonight was a bad idea I could feel it. Ty had been trying to holler at me for some time now and I always let him down so easy but from the looks of things he wasn't taking no for an answer. I walked into the house and I knew It was going to be some shit I could feel it coming but when I got upstairs to our master bedroom Jackson was knocked out sleep. I got in the shower and put on my pj's and jumped in the bed and went

YOU DID ME DIRTY: YOU REAP WHAT YOU SOW!

to sleep. Tomorrow was a brand-new day which meant I could either go into my stores or I could sit at home and run my business from my phone or computer either or.

I woke up around 8 am and when I looked over to Jackson side of the bed he wasn't laying there. I grabbed my phone to see if I had any missed phone calls and I didn't have any, so I got up and went into the bathroom and washed my face and brushed my teeth. I threw on my rob and went down stairs to the kitchen to fix me some breakfast when I got down there, I saw Jackson office door slightly open and he was on the phone talking to someone so I stood there and listened something I wouldn't even do naturally.

"I said I'll be over there in a few shouldn't you be in class why you calling me anyway." Jackson said.

I couldn't hear what the other person said on the other side of the phone, but I could tell it was a woman because I know damn well Shelly crack head ass wasn't in nobody school. I pushed the door open and stood there with my hands on my hips and Jackson hurried and ended his conversation.

"Let me call you back a little later." Jackson said hanging up the phone.

YOU DID ME DIRTY: YOU REAP WHAT YOU SOW!

"Who the fuck was you on the phone with and please don't play with my intelligence and say Shelly because I know that crack head bitch not in school. So, what bitch you seeing now please make me fuck you and these hoes up." I said walking further into the office.

"I don't know what has gotten into you Myesha, but I was talking to my little cousin who was supposed to be in school." Jackson said with a smirk on his face.

"Jackson I'm done playing these games with you let me know when you ready to be serious about us. Remember I don't need you for shit I been a boss bitch and I'll forever be one after your ass is washed up." I said walking away from Jackson.

I walked into the kitchen and pulled out some eggs and turkey bacon to fix me some breakfast. Jackson came walking into the kitchen yelling as usual when he wanted to get his point across.

"Let me remind you Myesha you don't have to keep telling me what a boss bitch you was before me and what a boss bitch you will be after me. I wasn't on the phone with anybody I heard you coming down the stairs and I saw you on the camera standing there, but you're so quick to jump to conclusion about something." Jackson said walking towards me.

YOU DID ME DIRTY: YOU REAP WHAT YOU SOW!

"Jackson get the fuck on somewhere you smelled like a bitch last night. I know you fucking with someone I just need more proof and when I get it, I'm done with your ass believe that shit." I said finishing up cooking.

"I'll see you later on I got moves to make you going to check on your business's today or you sitting the house." Jackson said wrapping his arms around me.

"I don't know what I'm going to do today why don't we take a trip somewhere for about a week." I said laying my head on Jackson chest.

"I'll let you know I got shit to do why don't you take Amber and I'll pay for everything." Jackson said kissing my lips.

I didn't even reply I pulled away from him and put my food on a plate. Jackson knew he had fucked up because whenever I ask him to do something, he always make up an excuse about the streets it's like he never puts me first. I grabbed my plate and sat down at the counter and said my grace and ate my food Jackson was still standing there shaking his head and I wasn't about to pay him any attention. I felt the tears threatening to fall from my eyes. I quickly ate my food and washed my dishes and left Jackson sitting in the kitchen still I guess he was waiting on a reply from me, but he wasn't getting one from me.

"Myesha baby come on don't be like that come on let's talk about this." Jackson said to my back.

I kept right on walking and went up to our room and turned the shower on. I needed to check on my stores and made sure the inventory had come in and make some deposits to the bank for this month. I walked into my closet and pulled out a Gucci jogging suit and some Gucci sneakers. I jumped in the shower and washed my body I let my tears that wanted to fall hit my face. I thought about all the shit I had been through with Jackson ass from the beginning until now and even though I don't need him financially I need him physically. I got out the shower and when I looked in the mirror, I didn't like the person I had become over the last year my eyes were puffy and red from crying. I put a towel around my head and went into the room and put my clothes on. After I had my shoes on, I grabbed my Gucci glasses, my purse and keys to my 2019 S- Class Jackson called himself trying to do the his and her's thing. Shit like this used to impress me and make me feel like we were forever but lately I hadn't

YOU DID ME DIRTY: YOU REAP WHAT YOU SOW!

been feeling like me and Jackson wasn't forever, and it wasn't because of Ty.

Walking downstairs I saw the Jackson wasn't nowhere to be found but he left three stacks of money on the table with a note that I didn't even bother reading. I grabbed the money and threw it in my purse and kept it moving. I went into the garage and jumped into my car and let the garage door up as I was backing out a car that looked like Shelly car pulled up behind me. I threw my car in park and jumped out when I saw Shelly getting out of her car.

"What can I do for you Shelly?" I said gripping my two five in my hand just in case I have to blast this hoe.

"Where is my ex-husband at did he think he could ignore me and not give me my money for the month. What you holding that little shit for you not going to do shit with it." Shelly said.

"Bitch don't worry about what I'm going to do with this little bitch keep fucking with me and find out. I don't know where Jackson at check the block bitch but don't be coming around here demanding shit and move your little piece of a shit car so I can go where I need to go." I said daring Shelly to jump stupid.

YOU DID ME DIRTY: YOU REAP WHAT YOU SOW!

I jumped in my car and watched her get in her car as well and speed off. Once I knew she was gone I pulled out my phone and sent Jackson a text to let him know his ex was most likely on her way to the block to see his ass.

Me: Your ex-wife just came through here as I was leaving asking about some money. I don't know why she think she can just pop up here and demand some shit check your bitch before I do please, and she might be on the way to see you.

Jackson didn't reply to my text, so I went to boutique to check the inventory and take the money out of my safe. When I got there Nicole was helping a client out. I walked to the back and got on my computer that was in my office which I kept it locked because I was only here two times a week which was to check the inventory and take the money out the safe that Nicole put in. Nicole was the manager at my location on the east side and Rochelle was my manager at my west side location. I saw that all of my inventory had come in I didn't see any boxes so Nicole must have put everything away; I ordered some new shit I seen that wasn't on the website weeks ago. I loved having new shit in the store I was thinking about going commercial in my store reaching out to Gucci, and a few other designers to start selling

YOU DID ME DIRTY: YOU REAP WHAT YOU SOW!

in my stores. When I was done ordering the items, I wanted for both stores I grabbed the money out the safe, when I was about to leave Nicole came into my office.

"Hey boss lady I had put out all the new things that came in not sure if you seen them." Nicole said.

"Yeah, I noticed none of the boxes were back here, how has everything been around here this week lady." I said grabbing my key's and things.

"Everything been good we were a little slow last week, but we picked up this weekend, whoever had a party this weekend had these broads coming in and out buying up everything." Nicole said.

"I bet hell we are looking a little low on inventory, but I ordered for both stores I'm about to be out and I'll be back some time next week boo." I said walking out my office and locking the door.

I walked out the boutique and as soon as I got into my car my phone rung, and it was Rochelle I didn't answer since I was on my way to the store. I still hadn't had a text message from Jackson which was fine with me. Jackson better know he is skating on thin fucking ice with me and this relationship. I pulled off and jumped on the freeway and headed to my store on Livernois when I walked in, I didn't see Rochelle anywhere and the store wasn't packed at all matter of fact nobody was even in here for it to be a Saturday.

"Rochelle where you at girl, and why didn't you put up any of the new inventory." I said yelling walking through the store to the back where her office was.

Knock... Knock...

"Come in." Rochelle said.

When I walked in Rochelle office, she was crying I had never seen her like this, so I knew something had to be wrong with her. I walked all the way into the office and put my bag and keys down.

"What's wrong Chelle you ok?" I said rubbing her back.

"My cousin Tank got killed last night at a party they started shooting. Some niggas was fighting and then shots were fired my cousin was just there trying to enjoy his night and got killed in a cross fire." Rochelle said.

"Damn girl I'm sorry I was there last night but I didn't know they started shooting. If you need to leave you can go ahead and leave, I will take over from here boo." I said.

"Girl I'm no good for my auntie right now I need to work to keep my mind busy. Your good I know you have to do the bank drop

YOU DID ME DIRTY: YOU REAP WHAT YOU SOW!

so I will be fine boo. Thank you I really appreciate you." Rochelle said.

"You sure girl I can stay it's my store I don't have a problem running my store. Let me write your family a check for support from my business to help." I said pulling out my check book.

"Thank you so much I appreciate the support girl, but I'll be here I need my money." Rochelle said.

"Ok girl but if you need to leave just lock up and leave and close the store down. I ordered some new items and I'll grab this money and go boo, matter of fact let me put this inventory up while I'm here." I said going into my own office putting my things up.

I went and put my stuff in my office and grabbed the money out of the safe and put it with the other money I had that needed to go to the bank today. I felt so bad for Rochelle family especially knowing that her cousin got killed behind Ty and Jackson dumb ass but I was pissed because I didn't know they got to shooting in the club last night this was one of the reasons why I don't go out because for one Jackson don't know how to act and people can't never go out and have a good time. Right when I was done putting up inventory Rochelle was out on the floor helping clients and I went to back to the office and grabbed

YOU DID ME DIRTY: YOU REAP WHAT YOU SOW!

my items so that I could go to the bank. My phone rung and when I pulled my phone out it was Jackson calling, I started to let it go to the voicemail since it took him hours to text me back with his simple-minded ass.

"Yes, Jackson it took you long enough I been texted your ass." I said walking out the office with the phone stuck to my ear.

"Don't answer the phone like that where you at since you not at home." Jackson said checking me.

"For your information I went to my boutiques to pick up my deposits and to order inventory why is it any of your business. I said getting into my car.

"Myesha what's up with the attitude, but when you coming home, I want to take you out tonight." Jackson said.

"I'll be home in a few Jackson on my way to the bank." I said.

I hung up the phone because I was simply tired of Jackson and about 10 minutes later I pulled up to the bank, it was packed because it was a Friday so I know I would be here for a minute. When I got out my car after parking, I was walking to the door and had my head down because my phone was ringing. It was Amber I had run into somebody

YOU DID ME DIRTY: YOU REAP WHAT YOU SOW!

hard ass chest. I looked up and my breath got caught in my throat it was Ty who I had ran into by accident.

"My bad I wasn't looking." I said.

"Myesha baby it's cool." Ty said

"Ty will you stop look at that mess you caused last night. I keep turning you down and you won't stop." I said trying to hurry and go into the bank.

"Myesha I won't stop because I know you are my future wife. I'm going to let you go but you make sure you tell Jackson this shit is far from over." Ty said walking away.

I went into the bank after he left and did exactly what I needed to do with my banker that I used while I was on the west side. I have a banker on the east and west it was best for me to have it that way. I keep it that way because if I don't feel like driving east, I can just go ahead and handle it at the West side bank vice versa. When I left the bank on my way home, I called Amber ass to tell her the news. Amber picked up on the first ring amped as usual.

"Bitch I know you saw me calling why didn't you tell me they got to shooting last night I know Jackson told you." Amber said.

YOU DID ME DIRTY: YOU REAP WHAT YOU SOW!

"Damn bitch let me say hello first and I just found out because Rochelle cousin got killed at the bar last night and Jackson didn't tell me shit." I said pulling up to my house.

"Girl damn that's fucked up where you at let's go shopping girl." Amber said.

"I just pulled up at the house I went to the stores to check and order inventory and I had to go to the bank." I said getting out the car.

"Well I'll come by later on or just let me know I guess I'll tell Landon I'll have lunch with him." Amber said laughing.

"Bitch you going to have to fill me in later." I said walking into the house.

"Ok girl." Amber said hanging up the phone.

I walked into the house and Jackson was sitting on the couch in his phone as usual. He didn't even pay me any attention when I came into the house which was fine by me. I put my stuff down and went into the kitchen and grabbed a bottle of water and some fruit. I sat down at the table and turned the tv on my stories was on. Jackson walked in the kitchen with his phone in his hand.

"So, you still talking to Ty after last night huh Myesha what you think this shit is a game." Jackson said.

YOU DID ME DIRTY: YOU REAP WHAT YOU SOW!

I was confused but shocked on how he knew I saw Ty, but I don't know why because Jackson had eyes everywhere. "First off I didn't even know Ty was going to be in the bank I bumped into him by mistake not paying attention so who ever telling you shit let them know it was innocent." I said grabbing my water and walking away.

Chapter Four

Noimi

Last night was a close ass call with me and Jackson, I didn't even know his bitch was going to be in the club last night and not that I even gave a fuck, but I was being cool because Jackson was my bread and butter and he paid for my classes. I went home like he told me to do last night but he never came over to the house last night like he said he was which pissed me off. I was falling in love with Jackson and wanted Jackson to myself I wasn't about to keep playing the side bitch I deserved to be the main bitch. I woke up early today and didn't have a text or phone call from Jackson, but I had heard it was a shooting and a fight last night after I left. I had an early morning class today, so I was up had my breakfast and got myself together. It was Friday so since it was the weekend Friday was the last day of the week for me with my classes until Monday. I was enrolled in Wayne County Community College for the LPN classes. I wanted more out of life than dancing. I danced at the club on Thursday, Friday and Saturday and I worked as a CNA on Sunday, Monday, Tuesday and went to school on Monday, Wednesday and Fridays. I had a busy ass life, but I made time for

YOU DID ME DIRTY: YOU REAP WHAT YOU SOW!

Jackson because I loved what we had minus him having a bitch. I don't nag him about him and his bitch.

When I was pulling up to the school my cousin Sacc was calling me. Sacc was my best friend and we were first cousins on my mom side I didn't have too many other friends so me and Sacc rolled hard. Sacc for short Saccora. I answered my phone on the 5th ring.

"Hey, my best bitch I'm just pulling up to the school. I wish you had gone out with me last night bitch." I said.

"Girl Boogie wasn't letting me go anywhere last night girl, but I knew he was there. I heard what happened too with Ty and Jackson girl. When you get out of class let's go shopping." Sacc said.

"Girl it's always something I haven't spoken to Jackson since last night. Boogie don't run nothing girl and I will let you know because I work tonight girl." I said grabbing my book bag.

"Well call me boo let me finish making breakfast for fat ass." Sacc said.

"Girl you a mess Boogie going to fuck you up." I said hanging up the phone laughing.

I walked into the school and went to my Psychology class and then I had clinical's as well today. I sat down at the desk and pulled my

YOU DID ME DIRTY: YOU REAP WHAT YOU SOW!

books out and my phone alerted me that I had a text message. I pulled my phone out and it was Jackson texting me.

My Bae Jackson: My bad about last night boo I went right home after the club. I'll be to the club tonight to check you out have a good day at school.

Me: It's cool Jackson I know you had to go home to your woman. I'll see you tonight I'm in class so let me text you when I get out.

My Bae Jackson: Ok.

I put my phone up and jumped right into my class work. I was sitting next to this girl name Tonya if I recall she dates Big B she was cool, but I didn't really conversate with her outside of class. Tonya was always my partner in our lab projects.

"Hey girl how you been." Tonya said dripping in her Gucci.

"I been good girl, ready to get these last few months over with so I can stop working two jobs." I said.

"Girl two jobs ughh I'm only doing these classes because I know fucking with a drug dealer his life ain't always promised you know plus Big B said I need to do something other than shopping and sitting on my ass spending all his money." Tonya said.

YOU DID ME DIRTY: YOU REAP WHAT YOU SOW!

"Oh, ok I guess girl well let me finish looking over this stuff you know we have a test in a few. I got to make sure I get my shit together I can't be failing." I said looking through my books.

I wasn't feeling nothing Tonya was saying she was making it seem like she was only doing this to shut Big B up and to me that wasn't cool, like she was trying to hold on to her position in his life when everyday with everything that he do he is risking his life so that she can look good. Our Professor Johnson was going over a quick go over for our test we were about to have.

"Ok Ladies put everything away and pull out your number two pencils. This will be your last test before graduation good luck this will determine rather you walk across the stage or not." Mrs. Johnson said.

The test we were taking was an hour long, I had finished in forty minutes which was good. The test wasn't hard it was easy most of the things we had went over during our year here. I was glad this year was over now I just need to know if I passed the test or not. Since I was the first one done, Mrs. Johnson was grading my test. I sat and went over a few other things I had been practicing for the big test to see if I would get my license as an LPN. My phone was going off none stop; I knew it was nobody other than Jackson. I didn't have time to answer because I was in class which he knew that already. I kept right on studying so I would be ready I wasn't going to take a break and wait to go to boards I was going to take my test right after Graduation while everything was fresh on my mind.

"Mrs. Noimi, please come up here please." Mrs. Johnson spoke.

I walked to the front of the class room while everyone else was still working. I noticed she was grading a few other papers which meant half of the class was either going to pass or not pass.

"Well I must say I was a bit worried about you, but you stayed focused on what you wanted, and you passed with a hundred percent. Congrats honey you will be graduating in a few weeks your closer to becoming an LPN." Mrs. Johnson smiled while she spoke.

"Thank you so much Mrs. Johnson it was truly a blessing to have a professor like you to help me along the way." I said walking away.

I went back to my seat to grab my things as I was getting up, I saw Tonya was still struggling with her test, even though I wanted to help her I wasn't about to mess my chance up with moving forward. I tapped her shoulder and she looked up and smiled. "Good Luck boo you got this."

YOU DID ME DIRTY: YOU REAP WHAT YOU SOW!

Tonya mouthed. "Thank you." And I was walked out the class, as I was walking to my car, I grabbed my phone to call Jackson back. When I got outside Jackson was sitting in front of the school with a dozen of roses. I don't know how he knew I would pass my test, but he knew it was things like this that meant the world to me. Jackson had paid for my classes and everything I needed so I wasn't just doing this for me I was doing this for him as well.

"Congrat's baby let's go celebrate." Jackson said kissing my lips.

"How did you know I passed baby; I just got my grade." I said walking to my car with Jackson on the side of me.

"Trust me I knew you would make me proud." Jackson said opening my car door for me.

"Make you proud huh where we are going, I'm following you boo." I said with my window cracked.

"Just follow me it's a surprise." Jackson said.

"Ok." I said starting my car up.

Jackson walked back to his car and I waited for him to pull out and I followed behind him. I didn't know where we were going, we were on the express way. My phone rung it was Tonya calling me I

YOU DID ME DIRTY: YOU REAP WHAT YOU SOW!

answered on my Bluetooth making sure I pay attention to Jackson and where we were going.

"Hey boo how did it go with your test." I said making a left turn into a gated community.

"I passed boo thank God I was so scared." Tonya said.

"That's good I'm so happy nurse Tonya and Nurse Noimi ayeee but let me call you back so I don't get lost." I said.

"Ok boo let's meet up some time this week." Tonya said.

"Ok boo." I said hanging up.

I got off the phone and looked around the neighborhood, I pulled up on the side of Jackson in a drive way. I was thinking I know damn well Jackson didn't bring me to his home where he share with his girl, if so, I was about to nut the fuck up. I watch Jackson get out the car and he stood there waving me over to get out of my car. I sat there for a minute until Jackson yelled.

"Get out the car girl damn this not my home." Jackson said.

I got out my car after grabbing my purse and locking my door I know my face said it all, but Jackson was standing there with a smile on his face. I wasn't smiling I didn't have time for the bull shit so when I walked up to Jackson, I had my hand on my hips.

YOU DID ME DIRTY: YOU REAP WHAT YOU SOW!

"Who house is this Jackson I hope you didn't bring me to you and your bitch house." I said.

"Girl pipe down this is not my house come on let's go inside." Jackson said.

Jackson grabbed my hand and pulled me to the front door, he went into his pocket and pulled out a set of keys and unlocked the door. When I walked into the house my breath was knocked out of my chest this house was beautiful as hell. The house was already furnished but I still wasn't understanding what we were doing here. I had looked all over this beautiful ass house the master bedroom was to die for and the closet was bigger than my condo that I had downtown. When I was done exploring this house, I found Jackson in the kitchen with a bottle of Moet and two glasses.

"What we toasting to Jackson this house is so nice." I said grabbing the glass.

"We are toasting to new beginnings, you becoming a nurse and becoming an home owner." Jackson said,

"A homeowner what are you talking about is this my house." I said.

"Welcome home this is your home baby." Jackson said.

YOU DID ME DIRTY: YOU REAP WHAT YOU SOW!

I jumped in Jackson arms and kissed his lips, Jackson stripped me down to nothing and fucked me crazy right in the kitchen on the counter. When we were done, I felt nothing but amazing, Jackson was everything I wanted in a man, but the thing was he wasn't my man. I was sharing him with someone else, so I could only be happy with the time I have with him during my time.

Chapter Five

Shelly

I'm the one and only Shelly I used to be married to Jackson that is before he called his self-letting me go and divorcing me. I know it was all my fault as to why our marriage didn't work, I was too stuck on myself and thinking that Jackson would never leave me or find out my deep dark secret that I was stealing his product and getting high off of it. I guess I was wrong Jackson found out and made his side bitch his main bitch. Jackson gave me money once a month to keep up with my bills and the lavish life I still wanted to live after him. I was still getting high, but it wasn't nothing serious only a few pills. I called Jackson for some money and I guess he called himself cutting me off, so I pulled up on his bitch so that she can let him know I mean business and I want my fucken money. I wasn't going away that easy I knew everything about Jackson business affairs so if he knew like I knew he would give me what I want or I'm going to sing to the fucken boys. I picked up my phone and called Jackson one more time before going to every spot his ass be at.

YOU DID ME DIRTY: YOU REAP WHAT YOU SOW!

"What do you want Shelly damn you popping up at my house demanding money what's up?" Jackson said.

"You know what I want Jackson where can I meet you don't make this harder than it has to be." I said smiling.

"Fuck you getting on my damn nerves meet me at the outback on 12 and Gratiot and make it quick." Jackson said.

"I'll be there in 20 minutes top ex-husband." I said being funny.

"Bye Shelly." Jackson said hanging up in my face.

I was still sitting in my car outside of my house, I cranked my car up and pulled off to meet Jackson. I was vibing to the music and in my own zone. I knew it wasn't going to take me long to pull up to the outback because I stayed 10 minutes away from them, plus I needed to go into Walmart to get a few things anyways. I pulled right up and didn't see Jackson car nowhere in sight. I looked at my phone and texted Jackson to let him I was there.

Me: Jackson I'm here where are you.

Ex Husband Jackson: I'm pulling up don't be fucking rushing me Shelly with your begging ass.

Me: Whatever Jackson.

YOU DID ME DIRTY: YOU REAP WHAT YOU SOW!

I put my phone in my purse and I saw Jackson Parking I got out my car and grabbed my purse. When I got to Jackson car, he had a look on his face that was priceless, but he smelled like nothing but perfume. I knew for a fact he wasn't with Myesha but that was none of my fucken business.

"Are you going to just stand there or come the fuck on so we can eat." Jackson said.

"You got some nerve rushing me." I said following behind Jackson.

"Welcome to Outback how many is in your party." Waitress said.

"Just two." Jackson said.

"Right this way can I start you two off with something to drink." Waitress said.

"Can I get a double shot of Patron, a lemonade and whatever she want." Jackson said.

"Um can I get a glass of Moscato and a coke please." I said.

"Ok I will be back with your drinks take your time with the menu." Waitress said walking away.

YOU DID ME DIRTY: YOU REAP WHAT YOU SOW!

I continued looking over the menu to scan and see what it was that I was getting. I finally settled over the chicken alfredo with a half rack of ribs. I looked up and Jackson and he had thrown the shot back and was staring at me like he had a problem.

"Why are you looking at me like that Jackson." I said.

"Are you high Shelly because if you are, I'm not going to continue to keep paying your bills." Jackson said.

"I'm not high Jackson I kicked that habit what is your problem." I said appalled.

"Yeah I hear you Shelly I'm not playing with you let me find out." Jackson said.

"Are you guys ready to order." Waitress said.

"Let me get the chicken alfredo and a half rack of ribs." I said.

"I'll have the same thing but add shrimp in my alfredo." Jackson said.

"Ok I will have that out to you guys as soon as possible." Waitress said.

About twenty minutes later the waitress returned with our food and refilled our drinks. Me and Jackson didn't say anything else to each

YOU DID ME DIRTY: YOU REAP WHAT YOU SOW!

other we both ate our food in silence. When we were done eating Jackson paid the bill and walked me outside.

"Here Shelly don't make me have to fuck you up this should cover you for three months." Jackson said.

"Thank you Jackson I really appreciate this." I said hugging Jackson.

"Yeah, yeah you heard what I said Shelly." Jackson said getting in his car.

I watched as Jackson pulled off and I pulled off to go into Walmart to get some house products and a few groceries. Jackson knew what he was doing, one thing I can say was he was going to always have my back no matter what.

Chapter Six

Ty & Big B

Ty

"Nigga I can't wait to catch up with that nigga Jackson he think he can get away with the shit he pulled the other night." I said pissed.

"Nigga I told you to leave that bitch alone but no you had to be in her face. We don't have time for no damn beef or no damn war. We got money moves to make and fucking with Jackson is not going to do nothing but add more stress." Big B said.

"Nigga you acting like a bitch I said what I said and meant it nigga." I said walking away.

Yo this that nigga Ty and as you can see a nigga like me was still mad as hell about the shit that nigga Jackson pulled in the club the other night over his bitch. Now don't get me wrong Myesha was bad as fuck and had all her shit together she ducks was sitting lovely before fucking with Jackson. I knew Myesha from around the way, but

YOU DID ME DIRTY: YOU REAP WHAT YOU SOW!

she would never give me the time or day. This nigga Big B was acting like a straight up pussy like he was scared of Jackson and his crew, but I had something for Jackson bitch ass when he least expected it. My little nigga Tank had gotten killed when Boogie started shooting in the club. I was fucking with Tank cousin Rochelle who happens to work for Myesha. Rochelle didn't know I had a thing for Myesha because had she known shit would be ugly right now. Rochelle didn't even know I knew Myesha and I wanted to keep it that way. I had left Big B barber shop and headed over to meet Rochelle at her aunt house to take some money for the burial. When I pulled up the hood was crazy it was folks everywhere. I spotted Rochelle so I called her so she could come to my car.

"Rochelle baby come get this money I'm parked outside you know I'm not going in it's too many people over here." I said.

"Ok here I come baby." Rochelle said.

While I waited on Rochelle to come to the car, I thought about how Rochelle was solid as hell. She had been down for a nigga since day one. I never had to question her loyalty unlike my nigga Big B bitch Tonya that hoe had spread her legs to anybody with some money. I had hit that hoe on numerous occasions. That hoe gave some

YOU DID ME DIRTY: YOU REAP WHAT YOU SOW!

mean ass head, but I wasn't about to keep tricking with that hoe, so I let her ass go and now she got my nigga Big B all in love. Rochelle opening the car door brought me out my daze. I had my 40 Cal sitting on my lap, but when I looked up, I realized it was my baby.

"Wassup baby how you are holding up." I said.

"Not good baby, not good at all I miss my cousin he didn't deserve to get done like that. Have you heard anything about who did it?" Rochelle said.

"Baby things happen for a reason and you know I'm here for you. I have my people with their ear to the streets as soon as I find out something, I got you. Here take this cash and it's a little extra in there for you to get yourself together as well." I said handing Rochelle the money.

"Thank you baby you always got my back. I love you and I'm sure my aunt will appreciate anything given to her since Tank didn't have no insurance." Rochelle said.

"Anytime baby but I'm about to get out of here let me know if you coming to the house tonight." I said kissing Rochelle on the lips.

"Ok baby." Rochelle said getting out.

YOU DID ME DIRTY: YOU REAP WHAT YOU SOW!

When Rochelle got out, I watched her walk away and she had a fat ass on her. I pulled off and took my ass to the crib I was tired as hell and hungry as hell. I pulled up to the red light on Chene and looked over to my left and Myesha home girl Amber was right next to me. She looked over at me and turned her nose up at me I laughed this was bitch was bougie and mad because I wasn't checking for her rat ass, I bet if I threw some cash her way she would be plucking away like a fucking duck. I sped off and left her dumb ass in my dust I had a condo down at the river place right off the water. It was nothing major a little three-bedroom, three-bathroom condo with a basement something simple a nigga like me didn't have no kids so I didn't need a house. I pulled into my parking spot after pulling up to my garage. I only had a two-car garage and both of my sporty cars was in there since this car was my everyday car. I wasn't a show off like my nigga's Big B and Boogie they stayed flexing on these hoes where I sat back and chilled but don't get it twisted, I jumped off when it was time, my gun finger stay itching like right now.

Unlocking my door, I kicked my j's off and went into the kitchen I pulled out some wing dings and fries. I was about to kick back and cook me some food. Yeah, a thug ass nigga like myself cook

YOU DID ME DIRTY: YOU REAP WHAT YOU SOW!

a nigga got to eat. I went upstairs to my master bed room and pulled off my clothes and released my piss that I had been holding. I flushed the toilet and jumped in the shower. My phone was ringing but I wasn't about to get to answer it. Once I was done washing my ass, I got out the shower wrapped my towel around my waist and went into my room and grabbed some hoop shorts and a beater. I slid my feet into my Nike slides and grabbed my phone off the bed where I had thrown it. I see it was Boogie calling so I called his ass back as I was heading down stairs to cook.

"Wassup Boog." I said when he answered.

"Nigga where you been at shit is hot in the hood over Tank killing." Boog said.

"Yeah nigga I know I'm in the crib I just came from over his moms house dropping some money off. I suggest you lay low nigga before motherfuckers put two and two together." I said seasoning my chicken.

"Nigga lay low for what that shit was a mistake you know that nigga Tank was my nigga. I'm sick over this shit nigga I should come through and chill for a minute and bust your ass in some 2k." Boog said.

YOU DID ME DIRTY: YOU REAP WHAT YOU SOW!

"Nigga come through then I'm cooking some wings and fries I know your fat ass want some bring a few rello's too." I said.

"Bet nigga I'll be there in about twenty minutes." Boog said hanging up the phone.

I continued to season the wings and fries and put my oil on, I didn't use flour that shit was deadly, so I cooked my chicken without all that shit. I went into my man cave it was set up like a theater room, I had the chairs, the popcorn machine and all the game systems hooked up as well. Whenever the boys come through, we always chill down here instead of in my main part of the house. I picked up a blunt and rolled come Kush up. I went back upstairs to check on the food I had the chicken in the air fryer and the fries on the stove. I got out the containers and made up some ranch, ketchup and hot sauce containers to take down stairs. When I was done, I looked on my television that sat in the kitchen and saw my nigga Boog pull up behind my car, I went to open the door.

"My nigga you made it here quick." I said giving my nigga a pound.

YOU DID ME DIRTY: YOU REAP WHAT YOU SOW!

"Hell, yeah nigga I over by Tank moms' crib that's how I got here so quick, them niggas over there thick as hell his family." Boog said kicking off his shoes.

"Yeah nigga I know had Big B made his way over there yet." I said going back into the kitchen.

"Damn nigga you got it smelling good in here got a nigga starving. I seen that nigga Big B over there for a minute he gave Tank moms some cash. He said he was going to stop be here when he left there." Boog said.

"That nigga haven't called me and said shit I was with him earlier before I stopped by there, let me season some more chicken." I said taking out more chicken.

I seasoned up some more chicken while Boog was rolling up and smoking and typing on his phone. I made up some more containers and made up some more fries as well. Just as I was done, I saw Big B pulling up as well.

"Boog go let B in." I said putting the food on the plate.

When Boog left to open the door I made sure all the food was on the plates and I didn't need to take no drinks down stairs because I had a fridge down there that was loaded. Big B and Boog walked back into the kitchen laughing.

"Fuck nigga you in here cooking you didn't tell me you were going to cook." Big B said.

"Nigga I was only cooking for me when Boog called me and said he was coming through, but I'm ready to bust y'all ass in some 2k so let's go grab y'all shit." I said grabbing my shit going down stairs.

We all went downstairs and played 2 k and got high as hell for about four hours until Big B bitch Tonya started calling him like crazy asking where he was. Them niggas left and I took my ass to sleep I hadn't heard back from Rochelle since earlier which was cool with me a nigga was high and drunk as hell and feeling good at the moment.

Big B

This whole situation with Jackson had gotten carried away, Ty my nigga but it shouldn't have even gone that far. Now we lost one of our niggas Tank because Boog gangster ass started shooting in the club. I wanted one peaceful ass night it was my birthday and a nigga couldn't even go out and have fun without niggas acting a fool and over a bitch at that. I know it seem like I'm soft but I'm far from soft I

YOU DID ME DIRTY: YOU REAP WHAT YOU SOW!

bust my gun like everybody else. After chilling at Ty crib getting blowed and playing the game I was on my way home to my bitch Tonya. Tonya was always nagging when a nigga was out making moves in the street. I had to make Tonya take up some classes because her sitting at home all day doing nothing but spending my money and nagging me wasn't going to get it. Tonya was due to graduate from LPN school in the next few weeks, I was proud of her, but I knew she didn't take that shit too serious or at least I couldn't tell she did. When I met Tonya everything about her turned me on, she was a beast in the bed and in the kitchen. I wifed her up without even thinking about what the future was going to hold for us. I love Tonya but if she don't change her ways with all this nagging, I was going to leave her ass right where she was at. Pulling up at the crib all the lights was on, so I knew Tonya was at home waiting on me and it was going to be a long ass night. I parked in the garage beside her car and made sure the doors was locked. I went in through the kitchen because it was the closer than walking all the way around to the front door. When I walked in Tonya was sitting at the kitchen aisle drinking a glass of wine.

YOU DID ME DIRTY: YOU REAP WHAT YOU SOW!

"So, now you decide to come home after ignoring my calls, Byron. I don't understand I do everything you ask me to do instead you stay in the streets fuck with different bitches and come home late." Tonya said.

Rubbing my hands over my face. "Damn, Tonya I was at Ty crib and time got away from me. I'm home now so what's the problem bae." I said.

"You know what there is no problem Byron fuck you I'm going to bed." Tonya said throwing her wine glass walking away.

After Tonya left me standing there looking stupid, I cleaned up her mess. After all the weed and liquor, I had already consumed I know a nigga didn't need nothing else to drink, but I was stressed, I threw me about three shots of Patron back and went to go upstairs to our bedroom. When I got to our door, I noticed it was closed, I turned the handle it was locked, I didn't have the energy to argue with Tonya I took my ass to the spare bedroom and took a shower and went to bed. I will deal with her shit in the am, but for tonight I needed to clear my mind.

YOU DID ME DIRTY: YOU REAP WHAT YOU SOW!

Chapter Seven

Tonya

I was in my bed by myself as I was every night dealing with Bryon (Big B) dope dealing ass. I loved everything about Bryon he took care of me and I wanted for nothing, but the only thing he lacked off was loving me the way I needed to be loved. Bryon thought that buying me clothing, shoes, purses and jewels was going to keep me happy and quiet. I know I may come off as a gold digger, but I am far from that. I took the little classes that Bryon paid for to be an LPN, at first, I just did it to keep him quiet, but the more I got into the classes I actually loved it. I haven't told Bryon, but I wanted to work for real and go to school for RN and further my education. I wanted more out of life then what I was getting. I wanted to get married and have children with Byron, I knew he was my soulmate. I knew God had a way of putting two people together and I believe Bryon was it for me.

Today was supposed to be a celebration but it wasn't because I was celebrating alone. When Bryon finally came in, I went off on him was I wrong or was I just acting out of the way I actually felt. I was lying in bed I heard Byron turn the knob on our door to our bedroom,

YOU DID ME DIRTY: YOU REAP WHAT YOU SOW!

but I was so engrossed in wiping my tears that I didn't care that he had to sleep in the other room. I knew it in my heart that Byron was cheating on me with someone who I just didn't know who as of yet, but if I find out I'm going to show my natural born ass in Detroit. I cried myself to sleep of thoughts of being alone and really finding out Byron was cheating on me, everything weighed so heavy on my mind.

My alarm went off at 9 am and when I turned it off and opened my eyes, my head was banging from drinking all that wine. I heard Byron banging on the door, so I jumped up so that I could open the door for his irritating ass.

Opening the door. "Damn you don't have to bang on the door like that." I said going into the bathroom turning on the shower.

"Shut the fuck Tonya it's too early for your shit and I didn't sleep good due to you being petty locking the room door." Byron said.

I didn't even reply I jumped in the shower and cleansed the stress from yesterday's drama off my body. I felt like I was relieving some stress. Just as I was getting out the shower Byron was coming in the bathroom naked as the day he came into this world. Even though the sight of Bryon made me horny as hell and he had me wet as fuck just from the sight of him I wasn't fuckin with him at all. I walked

YOU DID ME DIRTY: YOU REAP WHAT YOU SOW!

right by him and put my clothes on. I threw on a pretty ass sun dress I had gotten from Forever 21 and I paired it off with some wedges. I grabbed my purse, glasses and keys and went down stairs I was about to go to the mall. I was meeting Noimi there for shopping and lunch out in Novi. I could hear Byron calling my name.

"Yo Tonya, I know you hear me calling you come up here and let me holla at you." Byron yelled.

I kept doing what I was doing, I grabbed a bottle of water and left right out the front door. I slid into the butter cream seats in my 2019 Porsche. I hit the push to start and my blue tooth instantly connected to the car radio system. The last song I was listening too was Monica new song commitment. As I was leaving out the drive way Byron was coming out the door that was connected to the garage. I hurried and pulled out while he was getting into his 2019 Caddie truck.

"Call Noimi." I yelled to Siri over the Bluetooth.

Ring, Ring, Ring, Ring.

"Wassup girl I'm about to be pulling up to the mall in about 20 minutes." Niomi said.

YOU DID ME DIRTY: YOU REAP WHAT YOU SOW!

"Yeah girl I'm about 10 minutes away myself, I was just leaving the house. I'll see you when you get there boo let me finish concentrating on this road. I was just finding out close you were." I said.

"Ok boo see you in a few." Noimi said hanging up the phone.

When I got off the phone with Noimi I was pulling up to the mall. I found a close parking spot right by The Cheese Cake Factory. I grabbed my purse and put my sun glasses on and made sure my door was locked. With every step I took I knew I was a bad bitch even on my bad days I made sure I looked good. I went on ahead inside the restaurant to get us a table. The wait here was always no longer than two or three hours.

"Hello Welcome to The Cheese Cake Factory how many is in your party." Waitress said.

"Hello, it will be two in my party." I said.

"The wait time is two hours what is your name so that I can put you on the list and get you a buzzer." Waitress said.

"My name is Tonya." I said.

"Ok your light will buzz when your table is ready." Waitress said.

YOU DID ME DIRTY: YOU REAP WHAT YOU SOW!

"Ok."

I was about to walk away when Noimi came through the door. She was glowing and looked so happy I mean she was always happy whenever I saw her.

"Hey boo we have a two-hour wait don't you look like your slaying today." I said giving her a hug.

"Girl you know I stay slaying whenever I'm not in those scrubs." Noimi said hugging me back.

"Don't I know well we might as well get our shop on until this damn thing buzz." I said holding up the buzzer thing they gave me.

"Let's go boo, I'm ready to shop." Noimi said.

We went from store to store shopping for the next two hours, buying everything we can buy. It was refreshing to have someone I could talk too. We had so many bags that we had to go put our bags in our cars by that time it was time to eat the buzzer had went off. It was still a few more stores I wanted to go in before returning home Byron still hadn't called or texted me so that showed me, he had an attitude. We finally had made it back into the restaurant and they had sat us in a booth. We ordered drinks and ordered our food; it didn't take long for everything to come we made small talk mostly about getting jobs and

YOU DID ME DIRTY: YOU REAP WHAT YOU SOW!

everything with working in the nurse's field. Once we were done eating, we paid the bill and left a tip Noimi was tired, so she left I continued shopping.

Chapter Eight

Amber & Landon

It was well in the afternoon and I was still laying around the house. I had been secretly messing around with Landon everybody thought I couldn't stand him, but it was the other way around. I was usually up by now, but the way Landon put it on me last night and this morning had me out like a light. Landon had left this morning promising to come back through and chill with me for the reminder of the night. It was cool, but I don't know where this is going to go, I'm going to just let it flow. I turned on the television to catch up on my shows The Little Women of Atlanta was on recorded on my tv. I yawned I felt myself dozing off, but my phone stopped all that action.

Ring, Ring, Ring….

I looked over at the phone and smiled it was Landon calling me, so I answered the phone.

"Hey bae what's up?" I said smiling.

YOU DID ME DIRTY: YOU REAP WHAT YOU SOW!

"Shit lil mama just checking on you, I'm out making a few moves and taking care of some things. You good you need anything before I come back through later on." Landon said.

"I'm good I don't need anything I was dozing off before you called me. I was laying up watching my shows you got me tapped out bae." I said.

"I didn't do anything, but I'll call or text you when I'm on my way back that way." Landon said.

"Ok be safe bae." I said.

"Always." Landon said hanging up the phone.

After hanging up the phone with Landon I decided to call Myesha to see what she was doing. Even though I was tired I always talked to my best friend on a daily. Calling her phone, she picked up on the first ring.

"Bitch what you are doing." I said.

Sniff, Sniff.

I heard something on the other end of the phone like crying. "Hello Myesha, what's wrong?"

"I think Jackson cheating on me I found a bank statement for a house mortgage. We already got a house, so I know we wasn't talking

YOU DID ME DIRTY: YOU REAP WHAT YOU SOW!

about buying another one we just got this one. Jackson doing something he don't got no business doing. I'm going to find out what it is he doing and with who." Myesha said.

"Wait girl did you just say Jackson cheating on you, girl he wouldn't do that he loves you. Maybe the house is an investment, or a surprise don't jump to conclusions boo." I said.

"Jump to conclusions bitch I found the paper work as well with a bitch name Niomi name on the deed. So again, tell me my Jackson is not cheating on me." Myesha said.

"Come again girl." I said.

"You heard what I said Amber let me find out Jackson out here living foul I swear he is going to reap what he sow." Myesha said.

"I'll be over there in an hour boo." I said hanging up.

I got up off the bed and turned the television off and jumped in the shower. When I got out the shower, I looked in my closet for something to wear, I found some Nike cotton shorts with the matching shirt. I grabbed that and my black Airmax out the box, I lotion my body down and grabbed a panty and bra set out my dresser. Once I had everything on, I grabbed my crossbody Gucci bag and my sun glasses my keys was down stairs. I went down stairs grabbed my keys

YOU DID ME DIRTY: YOU REAP WHAT YOU SOW!

and turned the alarm on after heading out the house. I jumped in my 2019 Charger and hit the dash getting to my best friend house. I had totally forgotten that Landon was supposed to be coming back over her so I knew I had to call him before he come over, I can just have him look under my rock for the spare key.

"Call My Lil Secret" I screamed to my Siri.

"Calling my lil secret" Siri repeated.

Ring, Ring, Ring…

"What's up bae everything good." Landon said.

"Yea bae everything is good, but I had to make a run with Myesha. I wanted to call you and let you know that if you look under the rock you can get my spare key. I will be home soon and just keeping the key I'll replace it." I said blushing.

"Damn a nigga get a key now that's what's up. I will text you when I make it to the house, I'll grab some food since you will be out that way you won't have to stop." Landon said.

"Yes, you get a key I feel we are moving in a good direction. Please grab something I hate stopping I was going to cook but seeing Myesha needed me to ride with her somewhere I couldn't." I said.

YOU DID ME DIRTY: YOU REAP WHAT YOU SOW!

"Ok well take care your business and be safe baby I'll see you when you make it to the house." Landon said.

"I will." I said hanging up the phone.

Just as I hung up the phone, I was pulling up to Myesha and Jackson house. Myesha was outside with all black on just like me but she had on leggings and AirMax. I laughed my girl know she stay ready; I knew what she was toting in that bag plus she had one on her hip. I already knew shit was about to get real. I jumped out my car while Myesha was pacing.

"Bitch you going to wear the side walk out sit down." I said.

"Fuck sitting down bitch let's roll I got an address you drive I'm too pissed to drive." Myesha said.

"Let's go then bitch I'm ready to ride what's the address." I said while getting back in my car.

"2445 3 Ponds Court I'm about to figure out who this bitch is she better be a family member or I'm cutting the fuck up." Myesha said pissed.

I put the address into my dash board and it 45 minutes away from Myesha and Jackson house. Whoever house this was that Jackson had purchased he was trying to make sure they stay hidden. I

YOU DID ME DIRTY: YOU REAP WHAT YOU SOW!

kept the radio off because silence was the key for this mission a clear head. I looked over at Myesha and she was on her phone texting away and I guess it had to be Jackson because her face was tooted up looking crazy as hell.

Landon

I was shocked that everything with me and Amber was moving so fast. Amber had me gone in the head I can't even lie baby girl was the truth and it wasn't even the fact that the pussy was good, she had a good head on her shoulders. Baby girl had dreams and goals and I wanted to make sure she achieved those goals. Amber wasn't like my ex Saccora that bitch was a sack chaser, anything moving with money she chased. Saccora and Noimi was cousins and Jackson was fucking around with Noimi I mean Noimi cool, but I keep telling Jackson I don't see how he could fuck over Myesha like that. This nigga Jackson put this hoe Noimi through school and just brought her ass a house, but Myesha was a certified boss ass bitch. I fucked with Myesha and I fucked with Amber the long way as well. My ex Saccora started out as a fuck thing but feelings got in the way. Shit was cool in the beginning with us, but I started noticing her hoeish

YOU DID ME DIRTY: YOU REAP WHAT YOU SOW!

ways. I know she is fucking with the help Boogie, but that shit don't faze me hoes can't be taken seriously.

Me and Amber been rocking for a few months and shit been cool as hell. I enjoyed her company and our conversations, when she just called me to let me know she was riding with Myesha that shit spoke volumes to me. I was just pulling up to the spot and Jackson and Josh was standing outside talking. I jumped out my truck and headed to the porch where my boys was.

"My nigga bout time you got here you finally climbed up out that pussy huh." Jackson said laughing.

"Nigga you got jokes huh just the other day I couldn't get you up out of Niomi pussy so who is the joke on." I said dapping Jackson up then Josh.

"Both of you niggas pussy whipped." Josh said cracking a joke.

"Nigga you wish you had some pussy to whip." Jackson said passing the blunt they were smoking to me.

"Y'all niggas is crazy as hell so what's going on, we got a drop this week is everyone ready." I said.

YOU DID ME DIRTY: YOU REAP WHAT YOU SOW!

"Shit nigga I stay ready are you ready, I'm going to have Peanut, Jack to be at the warehouse that night to get the drop and we meet with them and do the count to distribute." Jackson said necking a bottle of Patron.

"That sounds like a plan nigga we needed to change up things just a little bit. So, what's the word on this nigga Ty you know that nigga is not going to let this shit go." I said.

"Nigga I'm to the point where I'm ready to run up on them fools." Josh said lifting his shirt to disclose his pistol.

"Nigga we need to continue with business, I'm sure Big B got his niggas in control. We have never had any beef but if that nigga want beef then beef, we will give they ass. I'm just saying let them niggas cone to us don't go looking for nothing." I said.

"Nigga I been over the shit he got his ass beat and I'm good on the gun play if he want that shit. Everybody in Detroit know Myesha is off limits he did better going after Noimi." Jackson said.

"Nigga like I said if the niggas want it, they can get it I'm not going to sit around and wait on them niggas to come at us." Josh said.

"Josh my nigga you always so hot-headed calm down let this shit die down." I said.

YOU DID ME DIRTY: YOU REAP WHAT YOU SOW!

"Nigga fuck you." Josh said.

"No nigga fuck you I said what I said." I said.

"I wish both of y'all shut the fuck up." Jackson said.

I dapped up Jackson and Josh and jumped in my truck to go get some food and take it over to Amber house. I pulled up to Walmart to do a little shopping. I walked in and grabbed a basket; I wasn't the type to be cooking and shit I did mostly take out. I grabbed some stuff to make a salad, I grabbed two nice ass steaks and some bake potatoes. Just as I got the wine aisle, I bumped into someone.

"My bad I'm sorry miss." I said and kept it moving.

"Damn Landon that's how you do damn you couldn't spoke to me." Sacc said.

"Sacc I don't have time for your bullshit keep it moving my baby." I said and kept walking.

I grabbed the bottle of wine I wanted, and I noticed Sacc was still walking behind me. I tried to ignore her simple ass, but she was making it hard she kept following me. I turned around and went the fuck off on her simple-minded ass.

YOU DID ME DIRTY: YOU REAP WHAT YOU SOW!

"Sacc I don't know what kind of shit you on but stop fucking following me, don't you have a nigga go follow him, but keep your hoe ass moving." I said.

"Nigga don't worry about what I have whoever got you buying food and wine must be special, nigga you ain't never did no shit like this for me." Sacc said.

"Key word I'm doing this for someone special you a hoe with a lot of hoe tendencies." I said and left her right there hanging.

I grabbed some store brought cheese cake and some roses and got in line and paid for my items. When I was walking out, I felt someone eyes on me and when I looked up it was none other than Saccora and Boogie. I chuckled and kept it moving to my truck I wasn't worried about Boogie or Sacc I had my shit on me if shit got crazy. I pulled out of the parking lot making sure I wasn't being followed on the way to Amber house and I hit a few extra corners and noticed nobody was following me. I pulled up to Amber house and went right under the rock and found the spare key I put it on my key ring with my car truck keys. I grabbed the groceries and started cooking dinner for us and I had the wine on ice. While the food was cooking, I sent out a text to Jackson and Josh.

YOU DID ME DIRTY: YOU REAP WHAT YOU SOW!

Me: Ran into Sacc at Walmart and Boogie was with her; nothing happen just keep y'all eyes and ears opened.

Josh: I got you word.

Jackson: I got you I'm on it on my way in the house with Myesha now.

Me: Alright hit my line later.

I plugged my phone up and finished cooking, I had some lounging clothing here, so why the food cooked I went to take a shower and changed my clothes. I had forgot to text Amber to let her know I was here, so I did that and went turned on ESPN.

Me: I made it here my bad bae, I got dinner on too see you later.

My Future Wife: Ok baby and I'll be home soon.

YOU DID ME DIRTY: YOU REAP WHAT YOU SOW!

Chapter Nine

Sacc & Boogie

The look in Boogie face when he saw Landon told me that shit was going to hit the fan soon. I tried to stay out of Boogie drama, true he was my man and Landon was my ex boo, but shit wasn't serious especially not as serious as me and Boogie. I was with Landon for the money, that nigga had plenty of money but don't get me wrong Boogie had that cash too, but it was something different about my baby. I had talked Boogie into going to Walmart with me so I wouldn't be out shopping by myself, I never intended on running into Landon, see Landon didn't do the whole cooking thing, he was more of pick-up take-out kind of nigga. I know you heard earlier I'm Noimi cousin she like my best friend/ sister. Me and her did everything together you didn't see one without the other. My cousin had all her shit together she was fucking with one of the biggest drug dealers in Detroit Landon right hand man Jackson. I didn't envy my cousin, but hell she just finished school and was about to be a nurse. I didn't have shit going for myself other than stripping and chasing Boogie ass.

"Bae you ready to go." Boogie said.

YOU DID ME DIRTY: YOU REAP WHAT YOU SOW!

Yeah bae let's go home my feet hurt I'm just glad I got the night off." I said.

"Yeah me too when you going to stop dancing and take what we have serious I told you I got you." Boogie said.

"Bae, I don't like depending on anybody so when is Tank funeral." I said trying to change the subject.

"You trying to change the subject but its tomorrow bae you are going with me." Boogie said.

"Yeah I'll go with you." I said just as we was pulling up at my apartment.

Boogie brought the bags in and I got started on cooking dinner for us while he put up the other stuff.

Boogie

I was ready to let that nigga Landon have it he was lucky we was in the store in public. I already feel sick that I was the one who killed my nigga Tank it was an accident but had them niggas Jackson and Ty not been fighting over a bitch none of this would have happened. I been in a fucked-up space since the shit happened, the only thing that keeps a nigga grounded is my baby Sacc, she

YOU DID ME DIRTY: YOU REAP WHAT YOU SOW!

something different. I knew Sacc fucked with Landon and she was known for being a hoe, but she hasn't showed me any of those reasons to leave her alone, so I was rocking with baby girl. Once we got back to her apartment, she cooked a little dinner for us, while I smoked a few blunts and played 2k I was trying to clear my mind, tomorrow I have to see my nigga in a casket that shit is fucking with me something serious. I didn't even bother telling Big B and Ty I saw that nigga, but I bet he told Jackson and Josh about us seeing each other.

I had dozed off on the couch when I felt something warm on my dick. I opened my eyes and Sacc was on her knees giving me the best head in the world. I just laid my head back and guided her head with my hand on my dick. Sacc knew what a nigga needed that's why I fucked with her so much. I was on the verge of Cumming, and when I felt the nut rise in my dick, I shot my load in Sacc mouth.

"Damn daddy that was big load." Sacc said.

"Shit girl you got my toes tingling bring me a towel so I can rinse my dick off what you cook." I said.

"I made Fish, Spaghetti and a salad." Sacc said.

"Shit girl you be throwing down." I said wiping my dick clean with the towel Sacc brought back.

YOU DID ME DIRTY: YOU REAP WHAT YOU SOW!

Sacc had fixed my plate and we sat and ate and smoked a few blunts then I fucked her crazy like she like. When we was done fucking Sacc was knocked out snoring like usual, I had laid up half of the night we had a long day ahead of us tomorrow I finally dozed off.

Chapter Ten

Rochelle (Tank's Funeral)

Today was a hard day for me and my family we were laying my cousin to rest. I haven't been able to function since my cousin was killed at Big B party two weeks ago. Me and my cousin Tank was thick as thieves. I knew him dealing with Big B was either going to land him in jail or dead. My aunt Rose haven't been taking this so good Tank was her only son. Aunt Rose was my aunt on my mother's side, my mother Roxanna was my everything she had moved away from Michigan years ago because she couldn't fathom all of the killing that was going on here. After my father Rockele was killed my mother has never been the same. I hate that my mother had to come back home to bury her only nephew it was heart breaking. I was in my bedroom when Ty walked in with his suit and tie on. I admired Ty but I knew it was more to the story then he was telling me see I didn't go to Big B party because partying wasn't my thing. I worked on a daily my boss Myesha was everything I was trying to be as a woman. She gave a check for my cousin covering half of the cost for the funeral. I had been working for her since she opened up first location right beside Nicole. Me and Nicole was cool as hell too we got along most times me, Nicole, Myesha and her best friend Amber hung out together.

"Baby you almost ready to go." Ty said tying his laces on his shoes.

"Yea baby I'm ready." I said putting the finishing touches on my hair.

"I'll be down stairs waiting on you do we have to pick your mom up or is she riding in the family car." Ty said.

"She said she will ride with my aunt Rose to the funeral." I said.

"Ok baby let's go before we be late." Ty said.

When I walked down stairs Ty must have already been outside, I looked at myself in the mirror my eyes was red and swollen from all the crying I had been doing. I was a little on the pump side thick BBW I didn't have a flat stomach I had a little pudge, but Ty liked it. I had on a black Christian Siriano trouser suit with the see-through sleeves. It wasn't hot out and it wasn't cold out hell we in Michigan the weather was always funny. I paired my outfit with a pair of strappy

YOU DID ME DIRTY: YOU REAP WHAT YOU SOW!

Saint Laurent heels. I had my clutch and my Saint Laurent sun glasses to block my eyes from being seen. This outfit complemented my body to the fullest when I got outside Ty was standing outside his truck on the phone.

"Yeah meet us at Mama Rose house we on the way now." Ty said to someone.

I couldn't hear what the other person said but I can only guess it was none other than either Big B or Boogie on the phone. Tank friends had come through on making sure my aunt Rose had everything she needed and was going to be taken care of after the funeral. Ty grabbed my hand and helped me down the steps and helped me in the car. On the ride over to my aunt house Ty held my hand.

"You look stunning baby." Ty said gripping my hand.

"Thank you baby you look nice too and I appreciate you for everything being here and helping me get through this. I don't know where I would be at without you." I said.

"I told you I got your back baby" Ty said pulling up to my aunt Rose house.

YOU DID ME DIRTY: YOU REAP WHAT YOU SOW!

Ty got out and walked around to my door and opened it for me and helped me out as well. My aunt Rose and my mom was standing at the funeral car. It was so many people here at my aunt Rose house so many people showed so much love for my cousin. I noticed Big B and Boogie and both of their girlfriends standing with them. I didn't fuck with all these females I was cordial I waved and kept it moving. My mom and Aunt Rose got into the Rose Gold Royals Royce that Ty had gotten for today. Ty helped me back into the truck and we all followed the Family car to the church. The Church was called The Lord Is Our Savor Baptist Church on Dickerson and Mack. It was a high church the pastor who was doing the funeral was one called in to get the job done right Pastor Kenneth Kole. He has been our pastor forever since me and Tank were kids.

Getting out the truck I felt like a ton of bricks was holding me down. We all lined up to go in Ty was holding my hand we didn't have many family members it was mostly people my mother and aunt grew up with and Tanks friends. As we made our way into the church, I could hear the choir singing Better Days by Le" Andria Johnson.

"Sometimes it feels cold and you feel all alone but hold on better days are coming. It can be rough in this world I know it ain't

YOU DID ME DIRTY: YOU REAP WHAT YOU SOW!

easy but hang on in there better days are coming. You've seen good, you see bad, you've been happy and sad but just remember that better days are coming." The choir sung.

When we finally got into the church and I was standing behind my aunt and my mom, Big B and Boogie had walked my mom and aunt into the church. My Aunt rose couldn't handle seeing Tank in the Casket. You could hear her screaming and I lost it form that point on Ty had to hold me up.

"Ahhhh my baby, why my baby, my baby Tank Y'all killed my only son. Why y'all take my baby away from me." My Aunt Rose yelled throughout the church.

They had sat my aunt and my mom down and it was finally my turn to see my cousin. I gripped Ty hand hard as ever and then I felt someone touch my back and when I turned around it was my boss Myesha. I hugged her and she whispered in my ear.

"It's going to be ok just be strong." Myesha said just above a whisper.

When I got to the casket I turned and looked for Myesha she had returned to her seat which was three rows behind us. Ty was still standing and holding my hand, I put my hand over Tank hand, he

YOU DID ME DIRTY: YOU REAP WHAT YOU SOW!

looked so peaceful laying there in this white suit. He had an open casket with his shoes showing as well. My cousin was well put together the tears rolled down my face and I had lost it.

"Omg cousin I can't believe you left me here, wake up please wake up, please. AHHHH I need you Tank wake up how are we supposed to go on without you. Wake up." Oh my God I can't breathe please somebody wake my cousin up. I yelled and screamed.

"Come on baby, it's going to be ok come on." Ty said pulling me to my seat.

I had finally sat down and all I could do was rock back and forth and stare at my cousin in that casket. It wasn't a dry eye in this church, I looked to my left and Ty was crying so hard I never thought about how this would affect him, Boogie had to be walk out he couldn't control his self. My aunt was up at the casket fixing Tank clothing she had lost it my mom was standing by her consoling her. My mom had taken this rather easy I thought she would have lost it since this was her only nephew. The Choir sung more songs and then the Pastor began to speak.

"I say Glory to God today we are here to celebrate the life of Tank Ralphele Jenkins. I remember when Tank was born, I baptized

YOU DID ME DIRTY: YOU REAP WHAT YOU SOW!

him. I'm not going to say Tank lead by example because we all choose our own path, but what I can say about this young man is he made sure he came to church every Sunday with his mother. Tank made sure his mother was ok he made sure his family was ok. Tank was like a son to me I've been knowing this family for a long time and Mrs. Rose I want to say God don't make no mistakes. Tank is with our father up above he is safe now; he has no more worries. I'm not going to sit up here and preach a long sermon about the rights and the wrongs but what I will say is we are living in our last days. God is going to come back, and the question is will you be prepared when he make his way back. Will you have your life together when you come face to face with God. All I can say for the friends of Tank, Mrs. Rose is still here Mrs. Roxanna her sister is still her and Oh little Rochelle who has grown up to be a beautiful young woman is still here, they are going to need you more than ever now. After today tomorrow is what counts being there after today is what counts don't let the calls, text's or the visits stop after today. Make it count be there after today because tomorrow is not promised give people their roses while they are here." Pastor Kole said.

"Amen." Someone in the church said.

YOU DID ME DIRTY: YOU REAP WHAT YOU SOW!

"I want to take this time out to let the family have their final viewing before we close the casket and end this celebration. Please if you are not family please stay seated only family please." Pastor Kole said.

My aunt stood up and Big B stood on the side of her to help her to the casket, my mother and Boogie stood next and Ty helped me up. When we got the casket, I thought I was going to pass out, my aunt was taking it better than earlier, my mother was shaking that being strong was out the door.

"Ohhh my only nephew auntie is going to miss you, now who is going to watch after my baby, why did they take you from us you still had so much life to live." My mother wailed why Boogie carried her back to her seat.

It was my turn and it seem like all eyes was on me, I kissed Tank on the fore head and when I got ready to head back to my seat with Ty holding my hand I saw Nicole approaching and she was looking big in the stomach like she was pregnant. I didn't notice she was here until now and she screamed.

"Please don't close it please let me see him please." Nicole cried out.

YOU DID ME DIRTY: YOU REAP WHAT YOU SOW!

I stopped and put my hands over my mouth it all made sense now Tank was the guy that Nicole talked about all the time, but she never mentioned she was pregnant not to me or Myesha. I looked to the pastor and mouthed.

"It's ok!" I mouthed.

She ran her hands over Tank hands, "I love you Tank, we love you Tank I don't know how we going to get through this without you. I don't know how I am going to take care of this child without you. Please rest peacefully and save a seat for me." Nicole Cried.

My aunt got up and hugged Nicole and Nicole hugged her back where I had questions and needed answers as to why she never told me. Why she never reached out after she knew what happened knowing Tank was my cousin. I don't know if I was pissed off or happy to have a part of my cousin still here. My aunt Rose looked as if she knew all along about Nicole and Tank, I wonder how much she knew. Once the casket was closed the funeral was over and we all walked out to go to the cemetery. After we left the cemetery it was time for the repass and when I say that Big B, Ty and Boogie out did their self, it was so nice it wasn't ghetto like the hood repasses be. They had it set by the water at the Marina and it was so nice. Me and

YOU DID ME DIRTY: YOU REAP WHAT YOU SOW!

Ty had Went to change clothes my feet was killing me I changed into a sun dress with some Valentino Sandals. It was comfortable and Ty put on a pair of jeans and paired it with a Gucci shirt and some Gucci Sneakers. When we got back to the hall everything was in full swing by now the DJ was playing some oldies and my aunt and my mom was mingling with everyone. The first person I saw out the corner of my eye was Nicole sitting at the table picking over her food in the daze she was sitting with Myesha. I walked over to them and took a seat. The look Myesha gave me let me know this was a sore subject and to just be careful.

"I want to thank you for coming Myesha I appreciate all that you have done for me and my family." I said.

"No problem baby anytime." Myesha said.

I looked around for Ty I noticed how he never came over and how he kept looking over here I brushed it off and then I looked at Nicole.

"Why?" I said looking for an answer.

"Rochelle it wasn't secret, but can we do this another day." Nicole said.

YOU DID ME DIRTY: YOU REAP WHAT YOU SOW!

"No, we can do this today you were supposed to be my friend, my best friend at that, why didn't I know you were pregnant by my cousin." I said yelling.

Everybody stopped what they were doing and starred at us, but I didn't care. I was going to get the answers I needed and right now.

"Look it just happen me and Tank just happened my heart is broken all I have now is this baby and my baby don't have a father. What more do you want from me Rochelle I'm hurting just like your hurting fuck let me be?" Nicole said getting up.

My aunt Rose, my mom and Ty came over to the table Myesha got up and went behind Nicole I guess to comfort her ass. I didn't care if everyone heard what was said. I was hurt my cousin was gone and here my best friend show up pregnant by my cousin and didn't tell me she was fucking him.

"Now Rochelle you leave Nicole alone now is not the time to talk about family matters. I knew about her and Tank and I knew about the baby. I was going to say something, but it wasn't a right time hell Tank had gotten killed." My aunt Rose said.

"Your aunt is right baby you need to be there for Nicole instead of being against her." My mom tried to reason with me.

YOU DID ME DIRTY: YOU REAP WHAT YOU SOW!

"Look I don't want to hear a damn thing either of you have to say I should have heard this from Nicole." I said crying.

"You watch your fucken mouth when you talking to me, I am still your mother and Rose is still your auntie. You ain't too old to get your ass whooped and don't you forget it." My mother said.

I turned to Ty and his expression said I was wrong, but I didn't give a fuck. "You ready to go baby I have to get the fuck away from here and all these lies." I said.

"Yeah baby go ahead and go to the car." Ty said.

"Yep." I said grabbing my purse and glasses and leaving.

Ty must have stayed behind to speak to my mother and aunt and make sure everything was good with Boogie and Big B. When I got outside, I didn't see Nicole or Myesha anywhere in sight, I hit the lock and got into truck.

Chapter Eleven

Nicole

Tank being gone was like my heart being gone, I knew for a fact me showing up to the funeral and not telling Rochelle my situation was going to put us in a fucked-up situation. Rochelle was my best friend and we been cool ever since we both started working for Myesha. I had never kept a secret from Rochelle but me fucking Tank I didn't know how to tell her. When I found Tank had gotten killed instead of reaching out to Rochelle, I stayed to myself and sobbed all day. I would go out in the late afternoon after work and go visit Mama Rose. I had to know that she was ok she was so supportive of me and Tank relationship and she insured me that she would handle Rochelle when the time was right. Myesha was there for me when Rochelle blew up on me at the repass. I hadn't been myself since Tank was killed, when I was home all I did was sit in the dark, I was so use to Tank calling and texting me and popping up at my apartment. I was back home, and it was the day after the funeral I was home from work and sitting in the dark on my couch. I knew I had a life in me, but I couldn't bring myself to eat, or sleep I just wanted to see Tank walk

YOU DID ME DIRTY: YOU REAP WHAT YOU SOW!

through my door one more time. My phone ringing, I checked the phone and it was Rochelle I started to let it go to the voice mail.

"Hello." I said.

"We need to talk open the door." Rochelle said.

"Look I'm not in the mood for your shit can we do this another day please. I just want to be alone right now Rochelle." I said wiping my tears.

"Girl if you don't open this fucken door I'm not leaving until you do." Rochelle said banging on my door.

Bang…. Bang…. Bang…

I hung up the phone and went to the door and opened it. "You happy now damn." I said walking back and sitting on the couch.

"Why you got it so dark in here bitch it's not the end of the world. Women lose someone they love every day you not alone you got me, my aunt and my mom and Tank homeboys Big B, Ty and Boogie and most of all you got Myesha to help you." Rochelle said.

"Girl fuck you mean it's not the end of the world bitch my child won't have his or her father it is the end of the world. I know who in my corner, but it will never be the same without Tank no matter what everybody do now are we done talking because I'm tired." I said.

"No bitch we not done talking, why didn't you tell me?" Rochelle said.

"Because I didn't know how you were going to take me fucking Tank." I said.

"Girl we grown I would have wanted to know so that we could have been there for each other instead of finding out when they are about to close my cousin casket." Rochelle said.

"Your right and maybe I was wrong, but I was in my feelings I'm sorry." I said.

"You good heffa now how far along are you because you barely showing. How long you and Tank been fucking around with each other." Rochelle said.

"Girl I'm 5 months I find out what I'm having next week, and we been fucking around with each other for almost two years, but we decided to be together six months ago." I said looking the other way.

"Bitch you a dirty bitch two years damn you hid this good I wish Tank was here so I could cuss his ass out, but I'll go to the appointment with you." Rochelle said.

YOU DID ME DIRTY: YOU REAP WHAT YOU SOW!

"Good your aunt will be there too." I said.

"Good now bitch open these curtains and turn some lights on your going to be good." Rochelle said doing exactly what she said making it light in here.

Me and Rochelle talked for a long time she made sure I ate and made sure I was good and then she left. I took a hot bath and then I got in the bed but not before saying my prayers and kissing the last picture of me and Tank.

Chapter Twelve

Myesha

When me and Amber rode out two days ago after finding that information on the house that was in some bitch name Noimi name when we got to the house it was big and pretty. We sat outside until some bitch pulled up, she was bad as fuck and she look familiar like I had seen her before I just don't know where I seen her. She had gotten out her car and had all these bags like she had been to the mall, I didn't say shit that day, but it wasn't over. I went back home after taking pictures of her ass. When I got home, Jackson was home cooking dinner, I wasn't in the mood for his shit because I knew in my heart something funny was going on. I thought he might have been still sleeping wish his stank ass ex-wife Shelly but hell I hadn't heard from Shelly since she came by asking for that money I guess she found Jackson tricking ass and got the money she was looking for because she never came back by here which that was good for her. I wanted to wait until after I had supported Rochelle for her cousin funeral, boy didn't shit hit the fan at the funeral and the repass. Nicole showed up pregnant and blew my fucken mind with that secret.

YOU DID ME DIRTY: YOU REAP WHAT YOU SOW!

It was the day after the funeral, and I was sitting in the kitchen drinking a glass of juice when Jackson came in the kitchen and grabbed me from behind like I said I wasn't fucking with him.

"What's up move around Jackson." I said.

"Fuck been up with you lately the last few days you been acting funny fuck is wrong with you is it something you not telling me." Jackson said.

"Nigga I know you doing something you have no business doing. I can't take you right now and until I figure out what the fuck you got going on, I'm not fucking with you Jackson." I said putting my glass in the sink and walking away.

"Myesha you are tripping I ain't doing shit at all and you think I'm cheating come on now ma." Jackson said walking behind me.

"Stop following me, but since you won't let this go who the fuck is Noimi and why do you have a house in her name. I'll wait for you to answer." I said turning around facing Jackson on the steps.

"Man, what you are doing going through my shit Myesha." Jackson said.

YOU DID ME DIRTY: YOU REAP WHAT YOU SOW!

"Like I thought nigga I can go through anything in this bitch that I please now answer the question who the fuck is she." I said once again.

"My cousin damn you happy now." Jackson said turning around and leaving and slamming the door behind him.

"Stupid bitch I yelled." Walking the rest of the way upstairs.

I went into our room and grabbed me some Black Balmain jeans out the closet and a black polo shirt with my black timbs. I was going to get to the bottom of all of this bull shit with Jackson today. I had already had my shower for today I threw on my clothes and grabbed my keys and purse and was out the door, I had my fitted D hat on my head, and I was on my way to this bitch Noimi house Jackson cousin or so he say. When I got in brand new 2020 Blazer it was candy red with peanut butter seats the interior was sick. I pulled out my drive way and put this hoe address in my MapQuest. I pulled out my other phone and called Amber.

"Yes, bitch what's up." Amber said.

"Bitch meet me at that address this nigga Jackson think I'm playing with him talking about that his cousin." I said.

YOU DID ME DIRTY: YOU REAP WHAT YOU SOW!

"Bae who is that on the phone come give me a kiss before I leave." Unknown male said.

"Bitch who you got over there why do that sound like Landon." I said.

"Bitch I'll be on my way bye." Amber said hanging up the phone avoiding what I was saying.

I was about twenty minutes away from this hoe house and I was ready for whatever. I had finally pulled up to the same address and low and behold Jackson new 2019 Maserati was in the drive way and so was this bitch car. I was boiling on the inside and I didn't know what I was going to do if this bitch happens to not be Jackson cousin and be one his many side bitches. Granted I was a side bitch when we first got together but I didn't know I was one until Shelly called me did, I feel bad hell yeah, I did but I know there won't be no coming back after this if Jackson is cheating on me. I pulled out my other phone and texted Jackson.

Me: Where you go Jackson meet me for lunch let's talk?

Ten minutes went by and he hadn't responded to me, but he read the message which let me know some fuck shit was going on. I was parked about four houses down, but I had a good view of the house, finally Amber pulled up and got out her car and got into my truck.

"Bitch what you are waiting for." Amber said.

"I don't know Amber I texted Jackson and he didn't respond, and I been here for about twenty-five minutes." I said.

"So, bitch he didn't respond yet." Amber said.

"Nope he didn't." I said getting out my truck.

"Bitch wait." Amber said.

I got out my truck and when I had gotten one house away that was next door to this Noimi house Jackson and was walking out and the Noimi chick was right behind him he walked her to her car and gave her a hug and a kiss that was all I needed to see. I was pissed I was livid I took off running.

"Really Jackson your cousin huh." I said swing on him.

"Hold up Myesha I can explain it's not like that." Jackson said trying to grab my hands.

"Fuck you Jackson I do everything for you I give you my all and you out here cheating on me with all the history we have you buying bitches houses and shit." I said swinging on him again and turning to look at the chick Niomi.

YOU DID ME DIRTY: YOU REAP WHAT YOU SOW!

"Bitch who you are calling a bitch." Niomi spoke up.

"Bitch you better chill don't say shit to her." Amber said walking up on Niomi.

"Girl you don't scare me you on my property you and your bitch ass friend checking my man." Niomi said.

"Bitch your man." I said popping her in her mouth and popping Jackson as well.

"Check your bitch Jackson she just put her hands on me." Niomi said.

"Niomi watch your mouth don't disrespect my wife like that take your ass in the house or go where you are going let me handle my woman." Jackson said.

"Fuck you Jackson you was just fucking me now that's your wife nigga you sick." Niomi said climbing in her car and leaving.

"Jackson, we done this is over come get your shit out my house nigga you did me so fucken dirty for the second fucking time, I swear you're going to reap what you sow." I said walking away from Jackson and out relationship.

I got in my truck and sped the fuck off, Amber was right behind me I knew Jackson was doing me dirty I felt it in my soul. I

YOU DID ME DIRTY: YOU REAP WHAT YOU SOW!

was such a wreck I had to clear my face at the next red light so I wouldn't wreck my truck. I was done with Jackson and I meant it there is no coming back from this one here. I looked in the rearview and Jackson was behind us as well. I took off when the light turned green, I was tearing my dash up I was putting this dash to use in this truck. I had to get home before Jackson his ass wasn't going to have the last say so I'm not the young dumb bitch I was when we first got together years ago. I was a grown ass woman who learned when a man is not for you everything that goes on in the dark will come to the light I believed in that shit. I don't feel bad for snooping in his shit he left it around, so he wanted me to see it. I finally pulled up the house I didn't even bother going into the garage to park my truck. I jumped out the truck and Amber was pulling up jumping out as well and right behind her was Jackson.

"Myesha you good boo this shit don't look good on Jackson behalf. I'm going to have Landon talk to him about this bull shit." Amber said as I was walking into the house.

"I'm good boo go ahead and go home I can handle Jackson." I said.

"I'm not leaving you." Amber said going into the kitchen.

YOU DID ME DIRTY: YOU REAP WHAT YOU SOW!

I didn't even say shit else I went to our room and into Jackson walk in closet and started throwing all of his clothing out on the floor. I started with clothing and then started throwing shoe boxes, he going to regret cheating on me fuck I look like some weak-minded bitch. I was the total package mind, body and brains I had everything going on for myself I didn't need him for shit at all.

"Myesha baby where you at." Jackson yelled walking up the steps.

"If you come up here Jackson be prepared to either take your shit or take a bullet now you pick and choose bitch." I said still throwing out his things.

"Baby come on it don't have to be like this." Jackson said standing in the room looking at me.

"Get your shit and take it to that bitch house the one you brought for her or hell go back to the house you and Shelly shared with each other but get the fuck out my way before I bust your dumb dirty dick ass." I said pulling my strap out my clip that was on my hip.

"I'm going to let you have this shit, I'll be back tomorrow and we going to talk about this shit. We not over until I say we over Myesha I invested time into you, into us so I'm going to let you clear

YOU DID ME DIRTY: YOU REAP WHAT YOU SOW!

your head but I told you a long time ago if you ever pull a gun on me again you better use it." Jackson said turning his back.

"You bitch ass lucky I don't want to pull the trigger on you because you turned your back with your bitch ass." I said walking behind Jackson.

By the time we got downstairs Landon and Amber was standing there talking. Landon was shaking his head when he saw Jackson coming down the steps. That only pissed me off even more I had put my gun back on my hip. I was crying the tears was coming down I was pissed the fuck off. I couldn't believe Jackson made me look like a fool all over again.

"Fuck you shaking your head for Landon I bet you knew all about this bitch too." I said with my hands on my hips.

"Yo, Myesha this is between you and Jackson I only came over here to make sure you two don't do nothing stupid and to talk some sense into my nigga." Landon said.

"Please spare me with the whole you give a fuck speech." I said. Grabbing the patron and necking the bottle.

"Myesha boo come on let's go in the kitchen." Amber said grabbing my hand.

YOU DID ME DIRTY: YOU REAP WHAT YOU SOW!

Once we got into the kitchen, I could hear Jackson and Landon talking. I was pissed off I was still necking the bottle, but I wanted to beat Jackson ass and this Niomi bitch. I got up and walked back into the living room where Jackson and Landon stood.

"Jackson you think you can keep trying me and making me look like a fool. When we first met you were married to that bitch Shelly and never told me the only thing that saved you from my hands was because you were actually in the process of getting a divorce but this here is different nigga you had a whole side piece on me. Nigga I cooked, sucked your dick and fucked you good on a nightly and daily basis. What I wasn't good enough for you nigga." I said punching him in his face.

Jackson jumped up and grabbed my hands. "I told you to keep your fucking hands to yourself." he said grabbing me around my neck and pushing me up against the wall."

"Jackson come on man you can stay at my house take your hands off Myesha just leave and let her cool off." Landon said.

"Nawl nigga she want this shit she want to keep acting like she a fucken nigga putting her hands on me. I'm about to fuck her up tonight I don't give a fuck what nobody talking about." Jackson said.

YOU DID ME DIRTY: YOU REAP WHAT YOU SOW!

"Nigga fuck you let me I go." I said spitting in his face.

I knew that was a sign of disrespect, but I didn't have one ounce of respect for Jackson. He let me go to wipe his face and I took off running to the kitchen where I had put my gun down at. He took off after me and he caught me by my pony tail and he choke slammed me on the ground. Landon and Amber came running in the kitchen behind us. Landon had pulled Jackson off me and pushed him out the house. Amber was shocked all of this was happening.

"Bitch you know you wrong, but I can't blame you though." Amber said.

"Bitch I'm done with him please leave I need some time to myself I'll call you tomorrow." I said walking Amber to the door.

Landon and Jackson was still outside talking, I saw Jackson looking at me while I was standing in the door. Landon said something to Amber I couldn't make out because the next thing I know she got in her car and left. I closed my door and slid down on the back of it and started crying the hardest I ever cried in my life. I had finally got myself up off the floor and went into the kitchen and grabbed my gun made sure my alarm was on. I made sure I had the Patron with me I went upstairs kicked all of Jackson shit to the side and ran me some bathroom. I stripped naked and eased in the tub my body was on fire from Jackson choke slamming me, my hair was all over my head. I laid back in the tub and drunk straight from the bottle and cried until I dozed off.

Chapter Thirteen

Jackson

I don't know why the fuck I didn't follow my gut feeling knowing damn well if Myesha found the paper work she had the address to the house. I wasn't thinking I went to make sure Niomi knew not to say anything other than she was my cousin, but the thing I was too fucken late I stayed too damn long and Myesha caught my ass. I should have been paying attention and had Niomi meet me somewhere, but I was stupid. I never meant for things to get carried away back at the house, me putting my hands on Myesha I loved Myesha she asked me was she enough hell yeah she was enough for me, I was just a nigga with money living his life the hard way still tricking on these hoes. I'm glad my nigga Landon pulled me off Myesha when he did, or else shit would have been bad. I know I was in the wrong now I don't know what I'm going to do to get Myesha

YOU DID ME DIRTY: YOU REAP WHAT YOU SOW!

back in my life. I wanted to marry Myesha and I wanted her to carry my babies, but I know that shit is out the question now.

I was sitting at my nigga Landon house while he was over at Amber house spending the night. I had been drinking since I got here and Niomi had been blowing my phone up since earlier.

Niomi: Damn nigga you can't answer the phone since you got caught.

Niomi: Jackson where are you.

Niomi: Jackson come over now we can be together I love you baby.

Niomi Fuck you then nigga you aint' shit I was just using your ass.

Niomi: I'm sorry about please come back over and lay with me.

I cut my phone off this bitch was losing her fucken mind texting and calling me back to back. If she thought that was going to make me come back over there, she had to be crazy this bitch was losing her mind and the shit was funny I was drunk as shit. I called my ex-wife Shelly she was the only one who could talk some sense into me. She answered on the first ring.

YOU DID ME DIRTY: YOU REAP WHAT YOU SOW!

"What do you want Jackson do Myesha know you calling me." Shelly said.

Speech Slurring. "I fucked up Shelly I got caught cheating now she don't want to be with me." I said.

"Nigga you stay putting your dick in somebody I knew you was doing wrong. I know me and Myesha don't get along and you cheating on me with her, but nigga damn she deserve better I thought you was a changed man." Shelly said smacking her lips.

"I know she deserve better I am that better that's why she my life line, my life partner, Myesha is everything I need in a woman and everything you will never be. I love her and I'm going to fight to get her back." I said.

"Nigga if you called me to put that I'm not the woman for you in my face you could have called the hoe you was caught cheating with. I know what I was doing was fucked up but nigga I was a good wife to your dirty dick ass." Shelly said hanging up the phone.

"Hello, Hello, Hello."

I hung up the phone when I noticed she wasn't on the phone anymore. I was miserable as fuck without my woman and nothing was going to be right until I got her back in my life and was able to move

YOU DID ME DIRTY: YOU REAP WHAT YOU SOW!

back home and be peaceful if that meant getting rid of Niomi then so be it. Niomi was good I got her a house, a car and put her thorough school and she was good on the money tip at least I hope she put some of the money I was giving her up for a rainy day. It was Five am and I wasn't about to keep drowning myself in sorrow and play pity the fool. I know I shouldn't be drinking and driving but I was going back home and get my lady back. I jumped up and made sure I locked Landon house back up and I jumped in my car and sped all the way home. When I finally reached our house all the lights was off expect the one in the bathroom. I parked my car next to her truck and jumped out and unlocked the door, I had already unset the alarm from my key pad. Walking in the house everything was pretty much the same way it was when I was dragged out by Landon. I went upstairs to our bed room and Myesha wasn't in the bed, all my clothes was still on the floor. I walked in the bathroom and Myesha was laid out in the tub, the first thing I did was panic that maybe she took her life.

I ran over the tub and checked Myesha Pulse and she had one I let go of the breath I was holding in. I saw the Patron bottle on the floor, and I saw Myesha gun laying on the floor, but it was still in the holster. I grabbed a big towel out the lining closet and went back into

YOU DID ME DIRTY: YOU REAP WHAT YOU SOW!

the bathroom and picked Myesha up out the tub she steered in her sleep, but I dried her off and dressed her and put her in the bed and pulled the covers over her body. I went back into the bathroom and took a shower and put on some hoop shorts. I cleaned up the mess that was in the bathroom and put my clothing back in the closet by the time I was done it was seven am I climbed in bed behind Myesha and held her in my arms and went to sleep with the love of my life. I was sleeping good as hell until I heard Myesha yelling.

"What the fuck are you doing in my bed Jackson." Myesha yelled.

"Myesha calm down I had to come back home I couldn't be without you just those few hours drove me crazy, I came back home and you were in the tub passed out I thought you was dead and you had drowned or killed yourself." I said.

"Well I wish I had of died and I wouldn't be in pain right now from you cheating on me Jackson. How could you do me so fucken wrong. I loved you and gave you my all, my everything and you did me so fucken dirty." Myesha said.

"I know and I'm sorry I don't know what I could do to make it up to you. I promise I will do whatever I have to do to get back in your

YOU DID ME DIRTY: YOU REAP WHAT YOU SOW!

good grace. Myesha you are my life line partner and I love you so much." I said.

"You got to do more than buy me some shit to get back in my good graces nigga. You fucked up royally and I don't think I can forgive you. You say I'm all these things, I'm your life line, life partner, your wife and you love me with all of your heart, but you still go out and cheat on me why. I never did anything to make you cheat on me, I did everything I could for you. I never nagged you when you stayed out late, I never cheated on you, I cooked, I cleaned hell I didn't ask you for money. I was perfect so why did you cheat nigga once again." Myesha said.

"I really don't have the answer to why I did what I did, but if we can work on our relationship, I promise I will be the best man I can be. I'm willing to go to counseling whatever it will take." I said.

"I need time Jackson." Myesha said walking away.

Chapter Fourteen

Joshua

What's up everyone I'm Joshua I guess you can say I'm the one who is always ready to turn the fuck up. I stay ready and I'm always on my bull shit. You guys already know who I roll with none other than the infamous Jackson and Landon. Them my home boys and we go way back to the hood. I'm the youngest of the bunch but don't let it fool you I get down with the best of them. All of my niggas had somebody and I off to myself fucking all these hoes none of them meant nothing to me that was until I meant this one woman and I say woman because I know the difference between the hoes I fuck and a real woman. Well anyways back to this special woman who won't give me the time or day. Her name is Tajia Coleman, I met her one night in a bar she was with her home girl Monica. I was out having a drink I didn't have nobody to go home too or answer too so I was free to do whatever it is I wanted to do. Let me make a long story short

YOU DID ME DIRTY: YOU REAP WHAT YOU SOW!

about when I met Tajia and how her playing hard to get made me want to man up and made me really want her more than ever.

It was one winter night and I was sitting in the bar having a drink, we had a rough night at one of our spots that was robbed, and we took a major lost. Me, Jackson and Landon had to come out our pocket to our connect Enzo in order for our next shipment to be on time and expected without having to go to war. As I sat at the bar and is aw this pretty dark skin ass woman who was on the dance floor with this light bright ass woman. I sat back and watched baby girl dance until she got tired when her and her home girl returned to the bar, I'm guess for drinks I made my way over to her to strike up a conversation.

"Hey pretty lady can I buy you and your friend a drink." I said sipping on my cognac.

She turned around her and her home girl, but what caught my eye was her home girl licked her lips when she saw me. Tajia turned her face up at me, I guess I wasn't her type. She had me drawled in by her beauty, her darkness was that rich ass chocolate.

"Excuse me my name is not pretty lady it's Tajai and I don't need you to buy me any drinks I can buy my own drinks." Tajai said.

YOU DID ME DIRTY: YOU REAP WHAT YOU SOW!

"My bad I didn't mean no harm I just saw your beauty from across the room and wanted to buy you a drink." I said.

"Well thanks but no thanks." Tajai said grabbing her friend hand and walking away I'm guessing back to the dance floor.

I went back to where I was sitting in V.I.P by myself and finished off my bottle. I wasn't drunk, but I wasn't sober either I was just right a nigga had to watch his surroundings. I looked out on the dance floor and Tajai and her homegirl Monica was out on the floor still dancing. I put a tip on the table and left, one thing about me was I didn't chase no pussy, I had plenty of pussy if I wanted to fuck something. A few weeks had gone by since I was at the bar and met Tajai and her friend Monica and Tajai was still on my mind heavy. I wasn't doing much it was almost the holiday, so I had to shoot to the mall and find me something to wear. I got up and got dressed for the day since I would be out most of the day making runs. When I pulled up to the mall, I valet my truck. I was hitting store after store I only came to get a fit for the fourth of July, and I ended up just shopping because a nigga could. I ran into the Burberry store it was going to be my last store because my phone was blowing up. Jackson and Landon had called me to meet up and talk business.

YOU DID ME DIRTY: YOU REAP WHAT YOU SOW!

Walking into the Burberry store I saw a Goddess standing in front of me. I thought I would never see her again but here she was standing in front of me in the flesh. I didn't want to seem like I was checking for her even though I was, but I kept walking and started shopping. When I had gotten everything, I needed I got in line and she was standing in front of me. When the sales associate got to Tajai that was my chance to speak up.

"I got her things you can add them to my bill." I said with confidence.

Tajai turned around with her hands on her hip. "Excuse me, oh it's you again look I can pay for my own items."

"My bad Queen it's not that I don't think you can pay for your own items; I see a Queen who I wouldn't mind taking care of making my wife one day." I said handing the sales associate my card and my items.

"Your wife your funny what is your name Mr. I want to make you my wife one day." Tajai said.

"Well Tajai had you not been rude a few weeks ago when I saw you, I would have told you my name is Joshua Cunningham." I said.

YOU DID ME DIRTY: YOU REAP WHAT YOU SOW!

"Well Mr. Cunningham it's nice to meet you and thank you for my things." Tajai said grabbing her bag.

I grabbed my bag and walked behind her. "So, this is how you're going to act can I take you out to dinner or can we grab a bite to eat here in the mall." I said.

"I'll meet you at 8 tonight at The Cheese Cake Factory." Tajai said walking away.

I watched her walk away and what a sight it was before me. I went to the food court and grabbed me a sub from subway. I didn't want to eat too much since I was meeting my Queen for dinner tonight. I walked out the mall and gave the valet guy my ticket and he went and got my truck. I loaded my truck with my items and jumped in and sped away. I pulled up to the block and I saw Jackson and Landon standing outside, I don't know why we always standing outside instead of going inside. I jumped out my truck and made my way to the porch Jackson and Landon was sitting on.

"Damn nigga we been calling your block head ass all damn day where you been at." Landon said with the jokes as always.

"Nigga I was busy minding my business what's going on." I said.

YOU DID ME DIRTY: YOU REAP WHAT YOU SOW!

"Shit trying to get this nigga Jackson out of a funk Myesha caught this nigga up now he sick." Landon said.

"Damn Jackson that's why you are sitting there looking crazy like you lost your best friend nigga." I said.

"Nigga fuck both of y'all." Jackson said walking away.

Jackson was walking away to his truck when a dark blue truck came down the street at a slow pace. Before any of us knew what was going on, they opened fire on us. Me and Landon started shooting back I was hit in my arm, but Landon appeared to be fine. When the shooting stopped, we ran over to Jackson who was lying on the ground with holes in his body, struggling to talk and breathe at the same time. We picked Jackson up and threw him in Landon truck and sped away to Henry Ford Hospital which was closer to us than St. John. I didn't want to have to call and tell Myesha what was going on because it wasn't looking good.

Chapter fifteen

Myesha (A Tragedy Occurs)

I was sitting at home after Jackson had left for the day, I agreed to let Jackson stay here in the house we share but he must stay in the guest bedroom. I was checking in on my boutiques from home, I wasn't in the mood to even be in the presents of others. Nicole and Rochelle had both returned back to work, while they were away, I was at one store and Amber was at another store for me. I was drained from dealing with my stores and dealing with Jackson and his bullshit, I honestly don't know how much more I can handle. I had been feeling sick and drained so much lately I just took it as I was stressed and depressed about everything going on around me. I had fixed dinner a little early today, I had a taste for Mac and Cheese, Roast and Potatoes, Dressing, Greens, Corn Bread and Peach Cobbler. My phone was ringing off the hook I wasn't in the mood to be talking.

Ring.... Ring.... Ring.... Ring.... Ring.... Ring.... Ring....

YOU DID ME DIRTY: YOU REAP WHAT YOU SOW!

Grabbing my phone up off the table where I was laying on the couch. It was Amber so I answered hell whoever was calling had called back to back.

"Hello girl what you want." I said with an attitude.

"Myesha I need you to come to the hospital now." Amber spoke quick and fast.

"Girl slow down what's going on are you ok." I said sitting up.

"Look bitch get to the hospital Jackson been shot and it's not looking so good." Amber said.

"Oh my God which hospital." I said jumping up.

"Henry Ford hurry up." Amber said hanging up.

I jumped up off the couch and ran upstairs to our room and through on some clothes I was in my gown. I put my shoes on grabbed my keys, my purse and ran out the door. I jumped in my truck and took off to henry ford hospital it would take me about twenty minutes to get there from where we stayed. I felt the tears pouring out my eyes I didn't even realize I was I crying until I felt my face and shirt wet. Fifteen minutes later I pulled up to the hospital and threw the valet guy my keys and he gave me my ticket. Landon was standing outside talking on the phone barking orders I'm guessing to their workers. When Landon saw me, he got off the phone with whoever he was on the phone with.

"Do what I said shut shit down until I say otherwise, we will be in touch. Let me hit you back in a few." Landon said hanging up the phone.

"Landon what happened where is Jackson why you got all this blood on your clothing." I said.

"Sis before you go in there Shit is not looking good Jackson took a few hits, but we got him here quick as we could." Landon said grabbing my hand and walking me inside.

Walking into the hospital I felt like the air had been taken from my body. I felt like I was losing myself Amber ran up to me and wrapped her arms around my body just as she was doing so the doctor came out.

"Family of Jackson Capon." The Doctor said loud looking around.

"Right here Doctor how is he. "I said crying.

"We have him stabled, but it will be touch and go so we have to monitor Mr. Jackson he took a couple shots. The only thing I can tell you is to pray for him." The Doctor said.

YOU DID ME DIRTY: YOU REAP WHAT YOU SOW!

"Thank you, God he will be ok, can I see him." I said.

"You can see him, but I'm tell you the sight is not the best, visiting hours are over at eight thirty." The Doctor said.

"I'm sorry doc but I will not be leaving this hospital until you guys release him so please tell them to bring me a comfortable chair. Please point me in the direction Dr. Johnson is it." I said.

"Will do and yes, it is Dr. Johnson follow me please and you are." Dr. Johnson said.

This bitch was getting on my fucken nerves. "I'm Myesha Capon Jackson's wife now please point me in the right direction before I cut up in here." I said.

"Sis calm down please." Landon said.

Josh came walking from the back with his arm in a sling and he had a scrawl on his face. I knew that shit was about to hit the fan behind this shooting, but right now I needed to make sure that Jackson was good. Josh walked up to me and gave me a hug.

"Sis you good." Josh said.

"Yeah, I'm good how about you I see you caught one." I said Grabbing hold to Josh.

YOU DID ME DIRTY: YOU REAP WHAT YOU SOW!

I grabbed Josh good arm because I started feeling dizzy as hell and my breathing had started acting funny. I had to sit down and catch my breath. I could hear yelling around me, but I was in and out of it for a few minutes.

"Mrs. Capon can you hear me are you ok." Dr. Johnson spoke to me.

I shook my head up and down that I could hear her. I was scared as hell because I had been feeling down for the last few days and I just chalked it up to me being depressed.

"We're going to have to check her in because she is not looking too good." Dr. Johnson said.

"I understand Dr. Johnson is there any way she could be close to Jackson. I know she wouldn't want it any other way but that way." Amber said.

"I'm sorry she can't be near him he is in ICU right now but as soon as we figure out what's going on with her and get her stabled then she can visit." Dr. Johnson said.

"Ok, thank you so much." Amber said.

YOU DID ME DIRTY: YOU REAP WHAT YOU SOW!

Chapter Sixteen

Boogie

I was amped as hell; I was feeling myself I had to bury my nigga Tank because I started shooting at Big B birthday party and I made a mistake and shot my homeboy. I'm the reason he in the dirt so because Ty and Jackson was fighting, and we lost one of ours one of theirs had to go. I saw Jackson bitch at the funeral I could have just snatched her up, but I was going to let her live she was innocent in all of this shit. See she tried to tell Jackson that night that shit wasn't that serious. I know what y'all thinking I pulled a hoe move, I lit they block up and I caught that nigga Jackson and Joshua hoe ass, I wish I had caught Landon hoe ass too then the competition would be over. Ty and Big B don't know what I did and at this moment they wanted shit to be over with and done, but nobody wanted to make no moves. I'm my own nigga I make moves when I want to make moves. I was back at the cut chilling with Sacc fine ass she had cooked a little dinner her cousin Noimi was over at the house chilling with her when I walked in.

YOU DID ME DIRTY: YOU REAP WHAT YOU SOW!

"What's up Noimi?" I said.

"Hey, Boogie how are you." Noimi said.

"I'm good, Sacc bae what you cook." I said.

Noimi had gotten up off the stool she was sitting on and grabbed her purse and keys. "Cuz I'm going to get up out of here I'll call you later maybe we can do lunch this week."

"Ok cuz you don't have to leave you ok." Sacc said walking behind her.

"Yeah cuz I'm good but the energy not good so I'm out." Noimi said leaving.

I was sitting on the couch laughing Noimi never could stand being in the same room with me and truthfully, I didn't give a fuck. I was fucking her cousin not her and I paid the bills here so she could leave ant not come back. I knew she was fucking with Jackson hoe ass, but that was a little pillow talking that Sacc did with me. Sacc told me all of Noimi business she didn't hold shit in at all. I went into the bedroom and got me something to slip into. I went to take a shower and when I came out Sacc was in the bedroom with a pissed off look on her face.

"Fuck wrong with your face bae." I said smiling.

YOU DID ME DIRTY: YOU REAP WHAT YOU SOW!

"Your what's wrong with my face, I mean my cousin don't like to be around you and where have you been all damn day. Big B and Ty came by here looking for you earlier." Sacc said.

"Look this is my house, I pay the bills here she don't have to visit hell go visit her if she can't take being around me. I was busy out making moves I don't owe you, Big B Or Ty shit I move when I want to move. Who the fuck you checking huh Sacc I take care of you." I said mean mugging her ass.

"You might pay the bills around here but nigga I take care of me, yeah you buy me a few items here and there but nigga I take care of myself. I'm not checking your ass if you ask me you can get the fuck on period. Let me find out you was on some bullshit I'm going to fuck you up." Sacc said.

"Fuck on somewhere Sacc I'm not about to argue with you where my food at." I said walking past her bumping her.

"Nigga fuck you get your own food." Sacc said walking in the bathroom shutting the door.

I laughed because she was a hot mess and in her fucken feelings. I went into the kitchen and fixed me a plate and heated it up. I grabbed

YOU DID ME DIRTY: YOU REAP WHAT YOU SOW!

me a juice out the fridge and sat down at the table and turned the tv on ESPN, my phone rung at the same time as the microwave beeping.

"My nigga tell me you didn't do what the fuck I think you did." Ty said.

"Nigga and what might that be." I said.

"Nigga you know what meet us at the spot in an hour." Ty said.

"Yeah ok when I'm done doing what I'm doing." I said hanging up the phone in Ty face.

I grabbed my food and sat down and started eating my meal, Sacc walked into the kitchen with her work bag and grabbed her keys and purse and left without saying anything to me. When she slammed the door I kept right on eating like nothing happened, one thing about Sacc is she will get over it she thinks the world resolves around her and I believe that nigga Landon got her feeling like that because he a sucker stroking ass nigga, but see I'm not that nigga we cut from a different breed. Once I was done eating I put my plate in the sink and went back to the bedroom and found me something to put on so I can meet with Ty and Big B hoe ass. I was getting tired of them and tonight I was about to let them niggas know it too. I put a pair of shorts and polo shirt with some airmax and grabbed my keys up and left out the apartment.

YOU DID ME DIRTY: YOU REAP WHAT YOU SOW!

I Pulled up to the block twenty minutes later and everybody was outside it was the first week of summer so all the hood hoes and hood niggas was out. I parked my car and got out I slapped hands with a few niggas and slapped a few bitches on they fat asses. When I made it in the house by it being a two family flat I went up stairs and knocked three times and the door came open. I walked in and Big B and Ty was sitting around the table smoking on a blunt and drinking a bottle of Patron. I took my seat without saying anything I had my eyes on them niggas because some shit was funny that these two niggas thought they could talk to me any kind of way like they started this shit by theyself we started this shit together.

My nigga you around here causing all kinds of drama for nothing." Big B said.

"Nigga what kind of drama I did what you two pussy ass niggas wouldn't do." I said.

"Nigga what I'm saying is I told you to let the shit go but you couldn't you went and did shit yourself making shit hot." Big B said.

Ty was just sitting there smoking and drinking not saying a word at all which was unlike him. I was tired of this shit so I got up and pulled my shorts up and proceeded to the door, when I heard a clicking

YOU DID ME DIRTY: YOU REAP WHAT YOU SOW!

sound. I knew coming here was an bad idea I went across the grain with this one, but Tank was my nigga and I felt bad as hell for shooting him so someone had to pay and why not the motherfucker who got this shit started. I didn't even bother turning around because I knew it was over.

Bang…Bang…Bang… Lights out everything went black and I went down.

Chapter Seventeen

Jackson & Myesha

You Reap What You Sow

It had been forty eight hours and I had finally woke up I looked around the room and it was empty not a soul by my bed but there were plenty of flowers, balloons and cards around my room. The last thing I remember was walking away from the spot on the way to get in my truck and then everything went black. I don't have a clue about what happened to me but seeing there is nobody here with me I'm guess I'll have to get the answers when the doctor or the nurse come into my room. What has me confused is no matter what me and Myesha went through I thought she would be here by my side, but I guess it really is over between us now. I tried to move and I was in pain, it hurt like hell, I pushed the button that was on the side of the bed I was laying in for some kind of help. A few minutes went by and a fine ass light skin nurse walked in the room.

"Yes, Mr. Capon you ringed, your finally up let me get your doctor so that she can answer any questions you might have. I'm your nurse for today I'm Nurse Jazmine." She said.

"Thank you Nurse Jazmine." I said

"Before I go did you need anything are you in pain or something." Nurse Jazmine said.

"Yeah I'm in a lot of pain but before you dope me up I need to figure out what happen and where my people at." I said.

"Sure the Dr. Johnson have all the answers for you." Nurse Jazmine said,

"Ok!" I said.

The nurse who name was Jazmine walked out the room and a few minutes went by and there was a knock on the door and Myesha walked in the room. She didn't look like herself, she looked tired and drained which had me worried. The look on her face wasn't a good one but you could tell she was here because she loved a nigga.

"Glad your finally up have you spoken to the doctor yet." Myesha said sitting down in the chair by my bed.

"Not yet I'm waiting on the doctor my nurse was just here though." I said trying to grab at her hand but she moved it back.

"Oh Ok well I'm sure she will be back with the doctor." Myesha said.

Just as I was about to say something the doctor and Nurse Jazmine walked back into the room.

"Mr. Capon your awake you nearly gave us a scare. I'm Dr. Johnson I was your doctor when you were brought in with numerous of gun shot wounds. I treated you and I treated your wife Mrs. Capon when she got here as well." Dr. Johnson said writing in my chart.

"Treated Myesha for what, what was wrong with her Dr. Johnson." I said.

"Well I will let her talk to you right now I need to make sure your vitals are good and check and clean your wounds." Dr. Johnson said.

"Ok Doc, how long do I need to be here I got things to do." I said.

"Jackson you will be here as long as you need to be here so sit back and shut up please and let them do what they need to do." Myesha said.

"Who you talking to like that Myesha just because I'm laid up in here don't mean shit." I said.

YOU DID ME DIRTY: YOU REAP WHAT YOU SOW!

"Mr. Jackson now is not the time for that please stop moving we are almost done. You was shot two times in the chest lucky that was all the bullets you took. They went straight through so you didn't have any damage at all, but we had to get you stabled you lost a lot of blood." Dr. Johnson said.

"Damn Doc that shit hurt." I said.

"We are all finished Nurse Jazmine please give Mr. Jackson something for pain." Dr. Johnson said.

"Well do Dr. Johnson." Nurse Jazmine said.

I looked over at Myesha she was all in her phone scrolling not paying me any attention. I was about to say something but Landon and Josh walked into the room.

"My nigga glad you up had a nigga scared." Landon said.

"Shit I see everybody keep saying that, Josh nigga what happened to your arm." I said.

"Shit I was hit too nigga but I'm good I was worried about you, I'm just glad your good. Sis what's up with you how you feeling since you been home." Josh said.

"I'm good Josh never been better look I'm going to run and get Jackson some food I'll be back." Myesha said.

YOU DID ME DIRTY: YOU REAP WHAT YOU SOW!

Myesha left out the room but not without rolling her eyes at me. I don't know what her problem is but I will get down to the root of the problem I know she couldn't still be upset about the shit from before. Landon got up and closed my room door while Josh sat down in the same seat Myesha was sitting in and Landon pulled up a chair for him to sit in.

"So, word is Boogie was the one who shot up the spot, but word is he was found dead two days ago." Landon said.

"So, you trying to tell me this nigga shot up our spot and now he dead. You, niggas took care of that shit quick and fast." I said.

"Nigga we didn't do shit a day ago Big B and Ty came to us on some let's dead the bull shit and came clean that Boogie took things on his own and did this shit. They both said they didn't want anything coming in between the business they had going on." Landon said while Josh was all in his phone smiling and shit.

"Wait so all this shit went down while I was laid up in the hospital. Josh who da fuck got you smiling so fucken hard nigga you haven't said a damn thing since you been here." I said.

Josh was about to say something and Myesha came back into the room with some food. Landon and Josh both got up and gave me a

YOU DID ME DIRTY: YOU REAP WHAT YOU SOW!

dap and hugged Myesha and told me they would be back tomorrow to check on me. When they left Myesha help sit me and moved my table in front of me with some cold water, some cold juice and what look like some mac and cheese, bake chicken, greens, yams and corn bread. I was happy as hell a nigga was starving. I dug right the fuck in when I noticed she wasn't eating at all she was scrolling through her phone not paying me any mind. I put my fork down and wiped my mouth with the napkin she sat on the table.

"Baby, I mean Myesha what's wrong why you not eating and why was you admitted into the hospital on the same day I was shot." I said.

"Look Jackson I had been feeling sick and drained when I got here to the hospital I passed out. They admitted me and I found out not only was I four months pregnant but I have breast cancer as well. I just want to make sure your good so I can concencrate on me and my body." Myesha said getting up kissing me on my cheek and leaving.

Myesha left me speechless on one hand I was happy as hell I was about to be a father, but on another hand my baby just told me she has breast cancer. I know first hand what cancer will do to you I lost my mother, my grandmother to cancer so I wasn't ready to lose

YOU DID ME DIRTY: YOU REAP WHAT YOU SOW!

Myesha to cancer as well. I pushed my buzzer for the nurse to come back to the room. When she entered she was smiling, it was a warm smile but I didn't need anybody distracting me from the real world I already had problems. I had to get myself well so that I could be there to take care of my Myesha.

"Yes, Mr. Capon do you need something." Nurse Jazmine said.

"Yeah could you heat this food up for me and bring me my pain meds please." I said.

"Yeah I can do that where did your wife go." Nurse Jazmine said.

"Look can you just do your job and stop worrying about my business thank you." I said.

"Excuse me Mr. Capon let me go and heat your food up and get your pain meds." Nurse Jazmine said walking out the room with my food.

I needed to figure out how to get out of here just as I was about to get up to try to use the bathroom, my phone rung stopping me in my tracks. Ring...Ring...Ring...

YOU DID ME DIRTY: YOU REAP WHAT YOU SOW!

It was my pops the Infamous Enzo Capon who happens to be our connect. I answered because if he was calling me then he was pissed pops never call me, he just send for me.

"What's up Pops?" I said.

"Do I need to send some help down there." Pops said.

"No pops everything is taken care of how you been though." I said trying to change the subject.

"I been good son just checking in with you how is my daughter in law." Pops said.

"Pops Myesha pregnant, but she has breast cancer as well. I feel like there is nothing I can do. I feel like I failed her as her man I mean I don't think I can handle losing her pops." I said.

"Well son you need to get well and take care of my daughter in law she will need you more than ever. You know I went through this with your mom so I know how your feeling." Pops said.

"Ok dad my nurse just walked back in here with my med hopefully I should be out of here by the weekend." I said.

"Good hit me up son." Pops said.

YOU DID ME DIRTY: YOU REAP WHAT YOU SOW!

I hung up the phone and Nurse Jazmine gave me my food and my meds. I ate my food and when I was done I dozed off them meds had me knocked out.

Myesha

I left the hospital emotional, upset and not knowing how to move forward in my life. Finding out I was pregnant made me happy because I always wanted to be a mother, but finding out I had breast cancer knocked the wind out of my body all in one night I thought I was losing my man, the love of my life, then I found happiness he was alive and stabled and I was pregnant then God said hold on I'm about to send you some mind blogging news you have breast cancer. I felt like I was coming and going on a daily because it was going to take some time for Jackson to get well and get out of the hospital. I didn't mean to hit him with a low blow like that but It needed to be said could I have waited until he was home yeah, but no I needed him to know what I was going through. When I got outside to my car I broke down and cried, I cried for the pain I am about to endure with carrying my child I am so far along, that the doctor is trying to figure out what is best for me as far as having the surgery to remove the cancer and being able to carry my son or daughter to full term.

Walking into our house I kicked off my shoes and went to our master bedroom. I walked into the bathroom and looked into the mirriol my eyes was puffy was all the crying I had been doing. I poured some levendar bath gel into the tub and threw in a bath bead and cut the water on to run me some bath water. I took off my clothes and looked the pudge that was forming in my stomach. I don't know how I missed this growth in my body. You know what they say as soon as you find out your pregnant you start growing and gaining weight. I slid down in the tub and the water felt so good on my body, I just let my body soak. My phone ringing the Bluetooth let me know it was Jackson calling.

"Hello, are you ok Jackson." I said into the phone.

"I'm good I'm calling to check on you bae, I know I did you wrong I get that, but I'm going to get out of here and take care of you and be the man you need me to be. I know what you going through and I am going to make sure you get the best care while you go through this. I need you to put Amber in charge of the boutiques and

YOU DID ME DIRTY: YOU REAP WHAT YOU SOW!

just take some time off and rest let's go visit my father and get a second opinion." Jackson said.

Before responding I took in everything Jackson had said to me and I knew he meant well that was one thing about Jackson he would put me before himself. I loved Jackson because no matter what he did he made sure I was good rather I needed it or not.

"Hello, you there Myesha." Jackson yelled in the phone.

"My bad yes I am here look Jackson I appreciate this I really do. I love you and I'm going to need you one hundred percent." I said.

"You got me baby go ahead and get some rest I'm going to get me some and when you get here tomorrow we are going to talk to Dr. Johnson about letting me out of here because your going to need me." Jackson said.

"Ok bae love you." I said.

"Love you too." Jackson said hanging up.

I got out the tub and got right in my bed naked I grabbed Jackson pillow and smelled his coglne and dozed off. It was eight am when I woke up the next morning I felt refreshed I got up took care of my hygiene and got dressed for the day. When I was done dressing I grabbed my keys, my purse, my glasses and got into my truck. I

YOU DID ME DIRTY: YOU REAP WHAT YOU SOW!

stopped to get us some breakfast on my way to the hospital. I pulled up to the hospital twenty minutes later and when got to Jackson room he wasn't in the bed and there was machines everywhere. I sat our food down on the table that was in Jackson's room and I went back to the nursing station to find out what was going on.

"Hey I'm Myesha Capon wife of Jackson Capon can you please tell me where he is because he is not in his room" I said.

"Let me get his doctor for you miss." The Nurse said.

She walked away and Dr. Johnson came down the hall way to speak to me. "Doctor can you tell me where Jackson at is there something wrong." I said.

"Jackson had internal bleeding late last night and he we lost him. But we got him back. He is in surgery now as we speak please we will let you know as soon as everything is over.

"CODE BLUE, CODE BLUE, CODE CLUE."

To Be Continued!